SELF-ESTEEM HABITS
FOR TEENS

How to Understand, Nurture, Accept, and
Embrace Your True Self

SAM REID

ISBN: 978-1-962496-01-8

For questions, please reach out to Support@OakHarborPress.com

Please consider leaving a review!
Just visit: OakHarborPress.com/Reviews

FREE BONUS

GET OUR NEXT BOOK FOR FREE!
Scan or go to:
OakHarborPress.com/Free

TABLE OF CONTENTS

INTRODUCTION

This book will not be very helpful to you unless you're completely committed to improving your self-esteem. Only you can change your life. And keep in mind that the journey to a healthier sense of self-esteem will not be an easy process. Your current lack of self-esteem didn't happen overnight and won't improve overnight, either. The tools needed for this journey are honesty, patience, and hard work.

With selected exercises that help you acknowledge what you have to give to yourself and the universe, you'll grow more confident every day. Once you've recognized your gifts, you'll be able to focus on developing positive self-esteem through joy, workouts, proactivity, meditation, optimistic visualization, compassion, ingenuity, and personal integrity.

What do you think self-esteem should mean to you? How fundamental should it be in your life? Your self-esteem is with you all the time. It could be your greatest support or your worst hindrance. It will either drive you ahead or drag you backward.

If you're always fighting with indecision and doubt, that's your self-esteem talking! What will your choice be? Do you want to be more assertive, or are you going to let life simply happen to you?

Your choice will determine the relevance of this book to you in the long run. If you choose to be passive on your journey, then you might as well drop this book right now and never open it again. If you choose to be assertive, then I give a big welcome to you!

It doesn't really matter how you got this book. Maybe your mom gave it to you as a gift, or maybe you bought it with your own money. It doesn't matter. I just need you to understand that reading this book will change your life for the better — if you let it.

CHAPTER ONE:
UNDERSTAND SELF-ESTEEM

Self-esteem is a topic that relates to a person's strong sense of personal achievement or significance. In simpler words, self-esteem is how much trust and value you place on yourself regardless of the things that happen around you. Your self-esteem has an impact on your decisions, relationships, mental health, and general well-being. It also has an impact on your motivation. When people with a healthy, positive self-image can see their own talent and capabilities, this pushes them to take on new challenges with zeal and vigor.

Self-esteem can be a controversial topic. Some people refer to it as the key to all their success, while others think of it as useless mumbo jumbo. You must consider how relevant self-esteem is to your own life and what measures you need to take to strengthen it. It's important to distinguish self-esteem from self-efficacy, which refers to your belief in your ability to handle foreseeable events, behaviors, or skills.

The world would be fairer if a magic spell could offer you a deeper, healthier sense of self-esteem. However, there is no such magic—no words of praise from anyone can give you significant, long-term self-esteem. Finally, this book has no phrases, activities, or pointers that will automatically fix you unless you want them to and do the work yourself. There is no quick fix. It's a loss on your part if you read this guide without undertaking the included activities (which, believe me, are hard but not impossible).

Self-esteem is as extensive as the wilderness, as dark as the coral reefs, and as ephemeral as the waves. Developing personal milestones, working diligently with your plan of action, and focusing on the relevant factors in your own life are all ways to boost your self-esteem.

How Does Self-Esteem Develop?

For decades, self-esteem has been a popular focus of modern psychology. It's something that's frequently addressed in therapy. We often use flowery and shallow language to discuss it, even though there is a wealth of research on the subject. Self-esteem is influenced by genetics, upbringing, life disappointments, peer group structure, and — most notably — our convictions.

At around two or three years old, our brains cultivate the capacity to understand other people's perceptions (both visually and mentally). The medial prefrontal cortex (mPFC) tends to grow at this point in our lives. The mPFC is essential for self-identity, individual awareness, and theory of mind. As a result, the mPFC is an important region for understanding ourselves and others. This is when a child may develop an interest in spinning in circles but fails to recognize that not every visitor who enters the house shares the desire to participate. Around the age of four or five, children learn things about their environment very quickly, and they start to understand that two individuals living in different ways react to things and view things differently.

Hearing their parents talk negatively of others is one of the most typical scenarios that people in therapy think about in order to get to the bottom of self-esteem issues. A kid may readily assume that all people are critical when a parent figure talks badly about others. On the other hand, parents who focus on having a loving and cheerful relationship with their children boost their children's self-esteem during adolescence and adulthood. People who feel that the world is typically caring are less prone to suffer from distrust and anxiety.

Our brains cling to memories associated with unhappy feelings and situations, particularly those in which we feel uncomfortable, ridiculed, or discarded. The brain decides what memories are crucial in preparing for possible future catastrophes. In fact, bad experiences or disappointments are often called to mind three times more easily than good experiences, even with the tiniest of incidents. According to a study, the brain needs five good experiences to convince itself that one negative occurrence was a blip.

This might seem insignificant, but this is the basis of where high self-esteem and low self-esteem come from.

Understanding Unhealthy Self-Esteem

The demon of poor self-esteem emerges in your life at the most inopportune times and places. It might manifest as despair, dread, worry, or thoughts of complete unimportance. The demon knows no bounds and has its own mentality. It is unrelenting unless you manage to notice its approach, identify its footfall on your doorstep, and refuse its entry into your life. Unhealthy self-esteem can be subtle and difficult to detect at times.

Although many people have some idea of what unhealthy self-esteem is, it may not necessarily emerge in the expected ways. Some believe that those struggling with self-esteem are introverts who seldom leave the house. They think that those who fail at maintaining their homes, professional lives, and relationships are often immersed in self-destructive, self-sabotaging practices. This is absolutely not the case. True, a lack of self-esteem leads many individuals to be reclusive or have terrible relationships. However, visibly oppressed people are not the only ones battling low self-esteem.

Unhealthy self-esteem can infiltrate every aspect of your life. You are probably unaware of how many of your difficulties may be caused by unhealthy self-esteem. People who have low self-esteem are more prone to think negative thoughts and promote their own pessimistic perspectives. If you are a cynical person, you might notice your own negative behavior from time to time.

Here are some other instances of how unhealthy self-esteem affects people from all aspects of everyday life. Individuals with unhealthy self-esteem are more prone to:

- Pressure others and become domineering.
- Be crushed by little errors.
- Have limited resources.
- Incite domestic or societal violence.
- Focus all attention on their failures, shortcomings, and setbacks.

- Put themselves down, either jokingly or genuinely.

Unhealthy self-esteem can have a negative impact on your emotional well-being. It is critical to address your self-worth and get the necessary help. Building self-esteem takes time, but there are things you can do to maintain your mental health as you work on improving your self-esteem, which we will talk about in depth.

Recognizing Unhealthy Self-Esteem

People with unhealthy self-esteem can be found everywhere. They are attorneys, car mechanics, hospitality workers, educators, athletes, maintenance workers, and stockbrokers. However, there are several manifestations of unhealthy self-esteem, and people with unhealthy self-esteem can be classified as either rebels, victims, or imposters.

Rebels demonstrate poor self-esteem by acting out. They try to establish themselves by ignoring others. They are adamant about demonstrating that they're either above or impervious to the laws and restrictions that everyone else follows. They are infuriated by feelings of failure buried within.

Victims dislike accepting responsibility for their acts or emotions. They feel more comfortable blaming everything on an outside reason and see nothing wrong with throwing a pity party. Victims are often perceived as weak in their relationships because they frequently allow others to overpower them.

Imposters expend a lot of effort and energy to prove they're confident. They are, nonetheless, motivated by a strong fear of failure and a persistent need to prove themselves. Imposters are frequently competitive and compare their accomplishments to those of others.

In general, someone who has unhealthy self-esteem may:

- Act immaturely and have weak emotional intelligence.
- Engage in self-destructive conduct.
- Easily become agitated and lose their cool.
- Forego their personality in order to "blend in."
- Avoid uncomfortable events and realities.
- Take pleasure in the downfall or disgrace of others.
- Regularly condemn themselves and others.
- Act condescending and boastful.
- Have an excessive response when criticized in any way.
- Commit self-sabotage.

This list is only the tip of the iceberg. Many people who ignore their self-esteem issues develop deeper and darker tendencies. People with unhealthy self-esteem frequently express inappropriate anger toward others. When you're overwhelmed with hatred and negativity, it can be difficult to manage and even more difficult to decide where to direct that anger. People with unhealthy self-esteem can sometimes become violent for no apparent cause. Even the tiniest word of criticism might set them off on a rant.

They start blaming others for their predicament and are unwilling to take responsibility for the repercussions of their own choices. They have zero consideration for others because they have no respect for their own life. They can't imagine that other people have something to live for if they don't.

Finding Your True Self

Finding your true self may seem like a selfish goal, but it is a selfless process supporting everything we do in life. It's a process of peeling away layers that don't help us in our lives and don't portray who we truly are. However, it also entails a major act of construction—identifying who we want to be and passionately pursuing our particular goal, whatever that may be.

Finding our true selves is a question of acknowledging our inner strength while being open to our experiences. It's nothing to be terrified about or avoid, and there's no reason to be overly critical of yourself along the way. Instead, think of it as a way of getting to know yourself just like you would if you met a stranger.

Have you ever looked at your reflection in the mirror and seen yourself through someone else's eyes? Have you ever considered your life narrative as if it were someone else's? It's probably not something you do every day, but have you ever tried it? Have you ever thought that there might have more than one version of you?

Your "self" may contain multiple roles, such as mother or father, daughter or son, wife or husband, aunt or uncle, friend, explorer, seeker, instructor, learner, leader, or follower. You may not always be those things all the time as you switch between roles and environments. Even deeper, you have a private self and a public self.

This makes the problem of unhealthy self-esteem even worse. You see and react to the world around you differently when you are in public and when you're alone in private. Your background, environment, and value system all influence your various selves. This can take a big toll on you even if you don't see it. Having two identities may cost you effort, sincerity, and self-esteem.

Consider this simple example: Let's say you're at a party with your friends, and they want you to go out on the dance floor and dance a little. You might balk and shy away from this idea as a result of your terrible dancing skills or because you don't want your friends to make fun of you if you don't dance well. Whatever your reasons might be, the bottom line is that dancing in public is a no-go area for you. We can categorize this as your public self.

Another instance is when you are alone with a trusted friend or your family. Your first reaction to any exciting news and happiness might be to dance. At that moment, you don't care whether you're a bad dancer—there is no fear of your family criticizing your dance moves, and you feel no need to hide. At that moment, you're acting out as your private self.

This example might not be accurate to your life, but I'm sure you can relate. Who exactly are you? Who are you when you're behind closed doors, or you find yourself alone? Some say the real "you" comes when no one is watching. Are you the vibrant, lively person you pretended to be at school today or the quiet, gloomy person you pretended to be during a party last week? That is a question only you can answer. You might not have the answers right now, but there is one thing you can rely on—the real you is specific, unique, compelling, and significant.

You may be nervous about exposing yourself to the public for fear of being judged or shamed. To blend in with the multitude or, at the very least, avoid standing out; you might claim to be a person you're not. People with strong self-esteem have developed a way to merge the person they are outside and the person they are in private in a deep bond so that they are not different from one another. Are you your real self, or are you pretending to be someone else? Do you act in such a way that others will welcome, love, visit, and contact you, or do you care more about being true to yourself?

Your self-esteem weakens when you seek to be someone or do something for the benefit of others. You are aware of the internal struggle that happens when you go against your own nature. You see that your real self has been beaten, and your "public self" has won. When you learn to make the best of every self and attempt to act as your one true self as often as possible, your self-esteem improves.

Self-Esteem Check: Too Low or Just Right?

Your beliefs, connections, and experiences all influence your self-esteem. You need to understand the range of self-esteem and the advantages of having positive self-esteem. When you have healthy self-esteem, you feel comfortable and happy about yourself. You believe that you are worthy of others' regard. When you have poor self-esteem, you respect your opinions and thoughts less. You may be continually concerned that you're not good enough.

Based on your experiences, your self-esteem will change over time. It's natural to go through phases when you feel bad about yourself and moments when you feel great about yourself. On the other hand, self-esteem frequently remains in a spectrum that fundamentally indicates how you feel about yourself, and it improves even more with age.

Here's how to detect whether your self-esteem is low and why it's critical to cultivate a strong sense of self-esteem.

1. Do you place low importance on your own work or ideas?
   o Never
   o Rarely
   o Sometimes
   o Often
   o Quite frequently

2. Are you quick to disregard your abilities or achievements?
   o Never
   o Rarely
   o Sometimes
   o Often
   o Quite frequently

3. Do you obsess over your flaws or shortcomings?
   o Never
   o Rarely
   o Sometimes
   o Often
   o Quite frequently

4. Do you reject or have difficulty accepting compliments from others?
   o Never
   o Rarely
   o Sometimes

- o Often
- o Quite frequently

5. Do you often compare yourself to others?
- o Never
- o Rarely
- o Sometimes
- o Often
- o Quite frequently

6. Do you feel that you're not the person you've always wanted to be?
- o Never
- o Rarely
- o Sometimes
- o Often
- o Quite frequently

7. Do you find it difficult to make or stick to decisions?
- o Never
- o Rarely
- o Sometimes
- o Often
- o Quite frequently

8. Do you have a tendency to be excessively sensitive to criticism?
- o Never
- o Rarely
- o Sometimes

- ○ Often
- ○ Quite frequently

9. Do you experience anxiety or discomfort in social situations?
- ○ Never
- ○ Rarely
- ○ Sometimes
- ○ Often
- ○ Quite frequently

10. Did you answer the questions truthfully (with your private self and not your public self)?
- ○ Yes
- ○ No

(Answers of *Never*, *Rarely*, or *Sometimes* indicate higher self-esteem, while answers of *Often* and *Quite Frequently* indicate lower self-esteem.)

Self-esteem influences more than simply our perception of ourselves. It also shapes how we connect with others, our environment, and our happiness. You shouldn't have any difficulties in these areas if you have healthy self-esteem. However, if you want to improve your general quality of life, there is always an opportunity for development. An increase in self-esteem may improve your relationships as well.

Activity: Worksheet on Personal Qualities

Set aside at least half an hour of undisturbed quiet time for this evaluation. Complete the following questionnaire as truthfully as possible. You should respond to these questions based on how you actually feel and behave rather than how you believe you should feel and behave. Remember that there are no correct or incorrect responses, and your choices will only be seen by you.

You're wonderful because you're unique inside and out. Assess your personality, your abilities, the way you treat others, and who you are—inside and out. Then jot down some qualities you value in yourself.

ACTIVITY 1	
Describing my public personality	
Describing my private personality	
Things I can do that I'm proud of	
How I treat people in public	
How I treat people when we're alone	
Who am I truly	

CHAPTER TWO:
INFLUENCES ON SELF-ESTEEM

Your perceptions about the sort of person you are, what you are capable of, your strengths, shortcomings, and future aspirations may all have an influence on your self-esteem.

There may be people in your life whose messages boost your self-esteem. If these signals originate from someone you respect, you might cherish their opinion more. Your personality, as well as your life experiences and the community in which you live, will influence how you perceive these signals.

Racial discrimination and bigotry have also been shown to be detrimental to self-esteem. Hereditary qualities that aid in establishing a person's personality might also play a role. At the same time, life events are regarded as the most important factor. Our experiences frequently serve as the cornerstone for our overall self-esteem. For example, those who routinely receive critical or negative feedback from family and friends are prone to poor self-esteem.

Factors That Influence Self-Esteem

Your Upbringing and Childhood Matter

One of the most fundamental predictors influencing your self-esteem is how you grow up. Everyone you meet during childhood has the power to impact who you become, including your self-esteem, since your personality and everything else about you is still developing. Children who grow up in unstable houses, for example, often have unhealthy self-confidence and self-esteem and carry the weight of those experiences throughout their lives.

Like many aspects of childhood development, self-esteem results from nature and nurture. Children's biological strengths and limitations (nature) have an impact on their growing self-esteem, but so do their relationships with family and their social setting (nurture).

Moreover, challenging and stressful early life experiences such as childhood sickness, prolonged hospitalization, moving to a new location, changes in structure, traumatic events, and abuse can limit or overwhelm children's development and how they define themselves. Early relationships and interactions between children and guardians, friends, and teachers can have a big influence on how they view themselves and manage challenging situations.

The impossible-to-control events that come with the territory of being alive can mold and impact children's developing self-esteem, but they don't decide it entirely. Self-esteem is a dynamic system in the sense that how people perceive themselves is highly impacted by how others perceive and treat them. Though self-esteem is a self-evaluation, it is easily influenced by how children are handled and whether they have a positive perspective of themselves when dealing with others.

As a result, because parents and guardians are the people that children first form relationships with, they can help children build good self-esteem. No one in the universe is more essential to children than their parents and guardians.

Material Possessions

Some people use material possessions to boost their feelings of worth, which are closely related to their profession and income. Because material things often symbolize one's status in society, material items are one of the most significant elements impacting self-esteem. However, this only applies to those who believe that material possessions boost our ability to be accepted by others.

The unpleasant truth is that relying on worldly items is a temporary high until you get the next shiny thing. Rather than being trapped in this ungrateful loop, embrace living with less and focus on nonmaterial sources of joy such as family, friends, traveling, or even volunteering. Instead of getting more stuff, consider feeding your spirit to find true happiness with yourself.

Friendship

You begin to be impacted by your friends as you grow away from the primary influence of your parents. Consider how pleasant interactions with other people have influenced your self-esteem from infancy to the present moment. Your friends have a significant impact on your life, beliefs, and actions. One of the most significant characteristics of friendship during your developing years is closeness. This has two meanings — that you are relatively near enough in location to maintain the relationship and that you share values, preferences, and passions.

There is probably a commonality between the friends you had in the past and the ones you have now — they are similar to you. It's highly unlikely that you'll have friends with opposing views and ideas to your own. Sure, you might have friends who do things differently, follow other religions, or have different ideas than you. But at their core, your friends are often fairly similar to you.

As you become older, your friends become your primary source of support and counsel. This changes when you develop intimate connections, but your friends will always be your supporters, helpers, and defenders.

The Media

Our obsessive fascination with the media, whether it's social media, television, or print advertisements, also plays a role in our self-esteem. With ongoing pressure to appear and act like public figures, celebrities, and peers, easy access to social media is extremely detrimental to young brains.

The border between fact and fantasy can become blurred with so many confusing signals. A lot of people end up comparing their lives to those of television, movie, and music personalities. You might find yourself thinking, "Why can't my boyfriend be romantic like him?" or "How come my body can't be as perfect as hers?" These questions begin to shape your perception of self and your ability to operate in the world.

Unintentionally, you begin to think, *If John can have such an accommodating family and so much support, why can't I?* or *How come I can't be as attractive as Jessica?* These comparisons begin to weaken your judgment and erode your self-esteem over time.

Environment

A significant portion of your time is spent at school or home. Every area of your life, including your self-esteem, is influenced by your surroundings. Stressful and demanding situations can frequently contribute to poor self-esteem, such as bullying in school or pressure from your parents to get better grades. On the other hand, a supportive and productive atmosphere can boost your self-esteem and help you grow as a person.

There are so many variables that can have an impact on your self-esteem. Every aspect of your life can affect it, but *you* have the greatest power to make changes. To boost your self-esteem, start sending yourself positive signals about who you are and stop beating yourself up.

Understanding Self-Concept, Self-Image, and Self-Esteem

Self-Esteem vs. Self-Concept

Self-concept is a term that simply refers to our impression of ourselves. This understanding is established via a range of experiences with important people in our lives. Our understanding of our own conduct, abilities and distinctive characteristics is referred to as self-concept. Beliefs like *I'm a good listener* or *I am a kind person* are part of our self-concept.

Our self-perception is important since it drives our motivations, views, and conduct. It also has an impact on how we feel about ourselves, such as whether we're qualified to do something or worthy of a certain thing.

Our self-concept is especially malleable while we're young and still in the process of self-discovery and creating our own identity. As we become older and learn more about who we are and what's important to us, our self-perceptions become much more precise and ordered. At its most fundamental, self-concept is a collection of ideas about the self and the reactions of others. It gives an answer to the question, *Who am I?*

Self-concept is composed of three distinct components:

Ideal self: The person you want to be is your ideal self. This version of yourself possesses the characteristics or traits you want to have. It's the person you imagine yourself to be if everything went just as planned.

Self-image: Your self-image is how you view yourself right now. Physical features, psychological traits, and social roles are all factors in your self-image.

Self-esteem: Your self-esteem is how much you like, accept, and appreciate yourself. A variety of variables can influence your self-esteem, including how others see you, how you believe you compare to others and your position in society.

Our connection with others helps shape our self-concept. Other people in our lives, in addition to family members and close friends, contribute to our sense of self-identity, as well as stories we hear and books we read.

Self-Image vs. Self-Esteem

Self-esteem and self-image are inextricably linked since self-image influences self-esteem and confidence.

The distinction between self-image and self-esteem is that self-image is how you "see" yourself in your own mind—the image you have of yourself in terms of appearance and behavior. It involves your idea of how others perceive you. Self-esteem is how you regard yourself and is more concerned with the type of person you believe you are.

Self-image is just one aspect of self-esteem. A negative self-image leads to negative self-esteem. A person who has a favorable self-image feels better about themselves, and this leads to higher self-esteem.

Your perspective is not reality. Instead, it's your own internal concept of reality. Everything is filtered and colored by your mind based on your values and thoughts.

You may think you're compassionate, but others may see you differently. You may think a particular hat looks stupid on you, but others may think it complements you or makes you appear sophisticated. How you view yourself is critical because it influences your behavior, thoughts, and interactions with others.

People react to you either positively or negatively based on the aura you exude. Your self-esteem determines your level of confidence in relationships. If you believe you appear tired to others, you may, in fact, begin to feel tired. You will be more cheerful and feel like you can conquer the world if you believe you look fantastic!

Your personal thoughts and beliefs mold your image, and those personal thoughts may sometimes be blurred. If you have a bad self-image, you may be extremely critical of yourself, and you may also find it easier to listen to and accept unpleasant comments from others. This can quickly turn into negative self-talk. Take action now by putting an end to any destructive self-talk you notice in your life. Replace it with more encouraging thoughts and words. You'll be astonished at the alternatives that will open up for you.

It's as simple as dressing up in the morning and staring in the mirror. If you love the person staring back at you and think that you look amazing, your confidence in your attractiveness will show in how you carry yourself and project a favorable image to others. You'll be reluctant to trust someone who says you don't look nice and more likely to believe someone who says you take their breath away.

It works the same way when you're uncomfortable with yourself—you tend to appear awkward and draw attention to your flaws. You'll be quick to believe someone who tells you that you don't look attractive and less likely to believe someone who tells you that you look amazing.

Because your self-image is all in your mindset, that's all there is to it. We've discussed the distinctions between self-image and self-esteem, and you've learned ways to begin improving your self-image, which will develop your self-esteem.

Understanding What Determines Self-Esteem

Our self-esteem, in summary, is our own opinion of ourselves and our beliefs, and it influences how we behave. This perspective on self-esteem is founded on cognitive behavioral therapy (CBT), which focuses on teaching us that how we understand our triggers leads to how we think and subsequently respond to everything around us. Triggers may include circumstances, experiences, relationships, people, places, and events.

Consequently, CBT teaches us that what we believe and feel about ourselves causes us to behave in specific ways. We must keep this process in mind when we examine how our self-esteem develops, including why it might become healthy or unhealthy.

While we are very young, we prefer to view ourselves in terms of our physical attributes and position in life. For example, *I am a pretty girl; I am an older brother/sister;* or *I am the youngest child.*

But, with each day, month, and year, we experience a larger outlook on life and share more moments with other people. And as we get older, our experiences are more diverse, as are the individuals we connect with.

All of these events and connections have the ability to influence what we believe about ourselves and how we feel about ourselves. Why do we intuitively follow this trend?

It's through these life events and connections that we come to know and understand more about our own qualities, tendencies, strengths, talents, preferences, interests, and disinterests, and how other people perceive those same qualities and behaviors. We also learn what kinds of character traits, personal qualities, and skills are seen as important by other people in our lives and in the community overall.

We then react to these experiences with ideas, emotions, and habits. For example, we begin to develop thoughts and perceptions about:

- Who we are as individuals.

25

- Whether we appreciate, embrace, and support who we are as a person.
- Whether we perceive ourselves as valuable.

We will feel either favorably or badly about ourselves according to the nature of these ideas.

Arrogance, timidness, and obsessiveness are all personality traits that might increase our chances of developing low self-esteem. However, it's crucial to realize that just because you have a certain personality trait that can contribute to poor self-esteem, it doesn't necessarily mean you will develop a low sense of self-esteem.

So far, you've learned about various influences that shape how we think and feel about ourselves, and you've determined which of these things apply to you. Remember that while these things may have had a detrimental impact on you and your self-esteem in the past, they don't have to continue to do so in the future.

How Does Your Past Affect Your Self-Esteem?

Every experience in life has the ability to impact how we think about and, therefore, how we feel about ourselves. However, certain experiences are more likely to have a negative impact on our self-esteem since they might cause us to question ourselves and our talents, feel insecure or believe that the experiences suggest something negative about us.

Challenging, difficult, disheartening, or painful experiences include:

- Harassment.
- Parental breakup or divorce.
- Violence and abuse in your environment.
- Tragedies involving yourself or others.
- Medical conditions and harm to yourself or others.
- Breakups.

In your pursuit of healthy self-esteem, it might be helpful and necessary to look back at your past in order to truly understand some of your current behaviors, habits, and personality quirks. What children see and hear has a big impact on them. Those who are brought up with supportive and compassionate parents or those who witness generosity, tolerance, and kindness are more sensitive to the emotional states and well-being of others.

Your personality and self-esteem as a teenager are influenced not just by what you learn from your parents, guardians, and relatives but also by what you observe and experience from their actions. Your family has perhaps the strongest effect on the structure of your self-esteem and the way you evolve throughout your life.

People who grow up in a home that is not nurturing or with parents and guardians who are inattentive to their needs are more likely to develop low self-esteem later in life. You might tend to rely on others' approval, whether verbal or nonverbal, to show you how to behave. You're probably doing this unknowingly, and you might be unaware that you're being influenced by something that dates so far back into your childhood.

Remember the great teachers who've fostered, supported, challenged, and guided you to a healthy understanding of the world? Their names quickly come to mind whenever you feel confident about doing something good. It would be perfect if all guardians could be like that. You probably also remember people who made fun of you, insulted you and made you feel as if you didn't deserve to live whenever you experienced fear or trauma. These influences are holding you back on your journey to healthier self-esteem. They were molding many of your views about yourself, whether you realized it at the time or not.

That simple example shows exactly how and why your past matters to your self-esteem. You need to forgive them, forgive yourself, and let go.

Forgiving Yourself and Letting Go

Why is it so tough to move past your long-held beliefs about yourself? Why is it so difficult to believe that you can change? The most important catalysts are consistency and regularity. You've been repeating the same messages in your head for so long that you've started to believe those words about yourself. You may even trap yourself in your critical self-talk by recalling things you said about yourself in the past. How is this possible? How come you can clearly remember what you experienced so many years ago, but you have to stop and think while trying to remember what you had for lunch three days ago?

You see how repetition is the key. The fact is that you've never really let go of your negative self-talk from the past. Instead, you've provided it with a refuge at the back of your mind, and it knows exactly when to surface, rear its ugly head, and strike.

Even the laziest and dirtiest of us clean our homes once in a while, while the neat freaks clean daily or at least regularly. You clean your sheets, vacuum your floors, and clean the glass because you want tidy surroundings where there is space for you to thrive. However, all of us often forget to wipe up dust and clean the mirrors in our own minds. You might allow self-criticism, negative thoughts, and damaging decisions to take root for years and years, sometimes until they are practically impossible to remove. A clean mind, free of our previous bad decisions, promotes healthy self-esteem.

When you're scared, the ghost of the past shows up. It emerges when you are upset, afraid, or lonely. It follows you after you have failed to overcome a problem; it swings by like an old friend you'd rather not hang out with anymore. But since you've summoned up the courage and strength to order it to go away, it keeps returning to convince you of all the terrible things you think about yourself. This ghost of your past makes it tough to move on from choices you made a long time ago.

To achieve healthy self-esteem, you must first forgive yourself. You have to work on eliminating the negative voice within you. Focus only on the part of your mind that sees the goodness inside you.

Activity: Self-Esteem Experiences

Use the box below for this activity. Write out five experiences that have affected your self-esteem in one way or another, whether negatively or positively. Write out the thought that came to you during the experience, the thought that stuck with you after the experience, and how you felt along the way. It might seem like a lot, but don't get scared. Be calm, truthful, and mindful as you do this activity.

ACTIVITY 2					
E x p e r i e n c e s	Your thoughts during and after the experience	Your feelings during and after the experience	How you managed the experience	How you acted as a result	How it impacted your self-esteem
1.					
2.					
3.					
4.					
5.					

CHAPTER THREE: GETTING READY FOR THE SELF-ESTEEM JOURNEY

The journey to healthy self-esteem may be long and difficult. It will also be a path loaded with unrivaled joys, unexpected twists, and a breathtaking finale.

The first task is to prepare your mind by quieting your inner critic and rejecting your negative self-talk. You are the only one in the world who can silence your negative inner critic. Because the critic is in your head, no one else in your life can do this step for you.

Healthy self-esteem will be unreachable for you until that voice isn't center stage. Everyone has an inner critic, but individuals with low self-esteem are more likely to create room for their critic. In many ways, your negative self-talk limits you. It undermines your ability to accept constructive criticism without completely exploding in anger, and it makes it difficult to see your mistakes as an opportunity to learn something new.

You can't grow because that inner voice is constantly reminding you that you're unworthy of progress or improvement. It constantly compares you to those you consider better than you, people who you believe are smarter, funnier, more beautiful, and so on.

If you give it a chance, it can seem more compelling than your positive voice or the voices of people who love and support you. However, you can choose to silence the negative part of your inner voice or at least shut it out so that it doesn't hurt your self-esteem. Recognize your inner critic the next time it starts to bring you down with doubts. Tell that voice that you've heard it, but you disagree, and you will not be listening to it. This is the first step toward silencing your inner critic. Simply ignoring your inner critic will not make it disappear.

The second step to quiet the critic is to make a deliberate decision that the next time you hear the inner critic speak, you will respond with five undeniable, real facts about yourself. To make the critic be quiet, you can't let it have any authority. When your inner critic says something, focus on anything positive about yourself that you know to be true. Maybe you love the outfit you're wearing. Maybe you did a good deed. Focus on those positive ideas instead of the negative voice.

Finally, you will quiet the critic by starting to work on the areas of your life that you want to improve. If you think you talk too much, have a bad attitude, or aren't good at making friends, and you want to address these flaws, then making goals is the next step on your journey.

How Negative Talk Causes Low Self-Esteem

People fail to achieve their goals for a variety of reasons. It can be because of procrastination, not planning ahead, or simply choosing the wrong goals.

Low self-esteem is another of these reasons, and negative talk tops the list of ways that low self-esteem develops. Your inner critic or negative self-talk can also stem from low self-esteem in the first place, creating a vicious cycle. "You should have done better on your test," says the voice. "You should have been a better friend." You've heard them all. The "shoulds" are a huge part of your negative self-talk.

If you need a way to break your focus on your inner critic, tell it to stop talking: "Be quiet!" Saying the words out loud can make you feel more confident. Keep repeating the words until you can tell that the negative voice is losing its power. "BE QUIET!"

Defining and Assessing Your Self-Esteem

If you try to put a value on your life and base your self-esteem on the opinions of others, you're rejecting your originality. You're convincing yourself that having distinct characteristics is completely irrelevant. You're telling yourself that you're not a wonder and that you're not here on Earth for any particular reason.

Consider your current situation in life. What exactly is your great mystery? What have you done that no other individual on the planet could? "Hardly anything," you may say. Incorrect! "I've never gotten an award," you may say, or "I've never made a significant contribution." These things may be true, but maybe that's not your personal life goal. Those are not examples of how you're a unique person. They're not the gift you bring to the world.

The most vital point you can consider to improve and strengthen yourself is to acknowledge that significance is, at best, relative and must be weighed against society. You are the only person on the planet who can determine your own importance. Allowing someone else to do it is the same as killing your self-esteem. The issue with personal value is that no universal definition exists.

For some, value is found in money. Others define value as belongings, children, relationships, skill, integrity, loyalty, passion, dignity, or knowledge. Everyone's sense of how to determine their own worth is vastly different. Assessing your worth is as tough as calculating money when you have dollars, yen, pesos, euros, and pounds on the countertop at the same time. Which is more valuable to you right now? Which one will best fit you on your journey? Everything is dependent on your journey.

If you can move past the judgments of others, you will have the kind of self-esteem that others aspire to have. It's easy to become preoccupied with what other people believe or what they say about you, but this just means you're focusing on other people's ideas. You're allowing other people's opinions to influence your decisions, attitudes, habits, and — most crucially — the way you view yourself.

Have you ever made a choice that is vital to your life, with the only influence being what others thought of you? When you do this, it's impossible to avoid hurting your self-esteem. When you want others to approve of you so much, it causes you to suffer.

You have to assess your self-esteem to discover whether what you believe about yourself is truly genuine or whether you have simply convinced yourself of it over time based on what other people say. Maybe they persuaded you of your views, and you never bothered to disprove them. To change a belief that doesn't make sense, you must first understand what the belief is and how you came to hold it. Then you can try to unlearn it by questioning it yourself. Put together a list of these issues and work to face the truth of the situation.

Consider this example scenario:

Monnie always enjoyed dancing, but she never dances in front of other people now. One day, she mentioned how much she loved dancing to Winnie, her best friend. Monnie was laughed at for being overweight. Winnie told other mutual friends about how Monnie loved dancing, and they said that someone as overweight as Monnie would definitely suck at dancing. Monnie believed them and gradually stopped dancing even when she was alone.

Her mother noticed and asked why Monnie no longer danced. After much persuasion, she revealed what her friends had said about her and how it made her feel.

This is an excellent illustration of how the views of others can distort your own ideas about yourself. You can't change the past or what you felt at a certain point in time, but you can choose what influences your future decisions, ideas, and actions. You can decide between shackles and wings. This is the essence of having healthy self-esteem: You have a choice about what matters to you!

Developing a Positive Mindset

Positive mental preparation is essential as you embark on your quest for healthier self-esteem. To make it work, you have to harness the power of your expectations. You must program yourself to expect that the adventure will be worthwhile and forget about people who don't believe in you. Forget about security, worry, what others say about you, your history, your family, your partner, your best friend, uncertainties, shortcomings, and duties — forget so that you can make progress!

Allow the negativity to leave, and concentrate on only one task — thinking positively about what your life would be like if you began to fulfill your goals. How would your existence evolve? What might you achieve for yourself and humanity? What kind of brilliance would you bring to the table? How would this influence your self-esteem? Concentrate on that one question and let go of whatever is holding you back.

Not many people strive to embrace their own uniqueness. Few people anticipate diversity. Few people predict happiness, but you can defy the odds and expect amazing things. Train your mind to always see yourself and your goals in a positive light.

You might be used to emphasizing what you're missing rather than what you have. You might be preoccupied with sadness rather than happiness. You might be fixated on your failures and mistakes rather than the successes along the way. You might be obsessed with discomfort rather than satisfaction. You might concentrate on confusion rather than the goal. Do you see the pattern?

This task is to focus on what is truly yours: your life's purpose and goals. Finding your own goals may be difficult, but it will be one of the most satisfying things you can offer yourself. Your sense of purpose will come to you more easily if you honestly analyze your priorities, goals, and desires. Think about why you're going through this difficult journey, what you want to achieve, how you want to get there, and who you want to be when you arrive.

Positive and realistic beliefs can be a navigator that will guide you on your journey. When you have positive beliefs as a guide, they will help you get to the places you need to go in order to move ahead with what you want to build. The same is true for your core beliefs. When your core beliefs are realistic, they will direct you to think realistically about your experiences, your relationships, and yourself, allowing you to move through life in a positive direction. Your self-esteem grows along with these positive core beliefs.

Setting Realistic Goals

According to statistics, developing healthy self-esteem has practical, favorable outcomes when working toward definite, realistic goals. This is far more effective than simply repeating mantras and seeking approval from others.

A goal can be anything you want to own, become, or accomplish in your life. Goals can be monetary, psychological, health-related, academic, or personal. They might be short-term to long-term goals. They might be as simple as cleaning your desk on a regular basis or as complex as launching your own business.

Goal setting seems so simple because we do it all the time in our heads and even on a whim in the moment. But in reality, goal setting is a serious affair if you are passionate about improving unfavorable aspects of your life, striving for positive results, and developing healthier self-esteem. It's the blueprint that may take you places that only a few people ever imagine, much less explore.

One goal should not conflict with another. If you set a goal to spend more time playing with your younger sibling or helping your parents around the house and then set another goal to study as many hours as possible to get a better grade, you've made goals that contradict each other. Neither will be accomplished. This also means that a minor goal should not conflict with a major life goal.

For example, your primary life goal, the goal that propels everything in your life, might be, "I will never deceive or hurt anyone else to get ahead."

However, if you set another goal that declares, "I will become the best student (or enter the best school, win the best award, win every race or competition) no matter what the cost," this goal would be in direct conflict with your ultimate life goal.

Goals should include an action verb. You shouldn't start a goal statement with wording like "I want to..." or "I intend to...." These are unattainable targets because they lack passion and drive! Begin with phrases like "I am going to..." or "I will..." Can you tell the difference between the two? The first two are undecided. However, the latter two examples are certain.

Goals also need completion dates. Without time constraints to reach your objective, there is no drive, no urgency, and no sense of motivation to achieve that goal. Without a deadline, you risk implying that you're not fully committed to your goal.

Finally, all goals must be signed by you, which we will go over in detail during Activity 5 later on in this book. Your signature represents your dedication to the goal. It implies that you are making a personal commitment to yourself. It states that you want to strive toward this goal in order to achieve higher self-esteem.

Don't forget! Your goal must also be accompanied by an implementation plan. The implementation plan is sometimes referred to as targets. This is your goal's appetizer. This is the critical phase where you decide what methods you will use to achieve your goal. How do you intend to save for your dream dress? Will you take on part-time work? Do you intend to open a bank account? Are you planning to cut back on other expenses? How do you intend to save this money? What is your strategy?

This is where you need to be as specific as possible. These steps must be practical and achievable for you. You might need to start easy and work your way up or take small, consistent steps toward your larger goal.

Let's assume your goal is to buy the dream dress you've been eyeing through the glass while window shopping, all without having to ask your parents for money. Your goal-setting plan to make the money can look like this:

1. I will figure out the exact price of the dress.
2. I will determine the amount of time I want to save up the money.

3. I will decide whether I will save in a bank account or use a piggy bank.
4. I will find a way to save money, whether that's a part-time job or asking cutting expenses out of my allowance.
5. I will stick to my goal and save the money before the goal completion date.

Your own goal might be different, but for everyone, there must be a plan for how to achieve it. Someone who sets frequent targets and reviews their progress on a regular basis will be able to do more in a shorter amount of time and develop feelings of drive and focus. Setting a balance of short-term, medium-term, and long-term targets is also beneficial. Having too many long-term goals might be disappointing and frustrating without short-term targets to keep us inspired.

Setting Rewards for Each Completed Goal

Creating goals might be difficult, but setting targets and rewarding yourself makes it much simpler to stay focused and motivated! Make this bargain with yourself, and you will be successful with your goals!

Although not everyone sets goals with this same approach, everyone does something similar when they create lists. It might be a to-do list, to-buy list, must-watch movie list, or must-read books list. These can be daily, biweekly, monthly, annual, or continuous targets. They all have an impact on your life.

Sometimes, these objectives are simple. Take out the garbage? Check! Load the dishwasher? Finished! However, some objectives are extremely tough to achieve, such as a lifelong aim of embracing a healthier lifestyle. Why is this the case? One of the main reasons these long-term goals are so difficult is that there is no instant reward. It's depressing to work out and eat healthy foods for months only to see little change in your body. That's why celebrating smaller successes is important as well.

The reward for meeting a smaller goal doesn't have to be something complex or expensive. For example, if you'd like to stop drinking soda completely, it would be unrealistic to wake up one day and stop drinking it forever. It makes more sense to start by taking baby steps. You could set a shorter goal of two weeks and then line up a reward if you can stick with it. Maybe the reward is that the money that would have gone toward buying soda can go instead toward saving for new clothes. The longer you go without consuming soda, the more money you'll have for new outfits. It's that simple!

All you need to do is set a specific, realistic goal and identify a good outcome for meeting it. Make sure you follow through on your commitments and genuinely reward yourself. Your objectives should be difficult yet achievable. The goal is to push yourself to do better on the current target.

At the end of this chapter, try to set up a realistic goal for yourself and write it down. You should have something like this: "I (your name) recognize that I am always working on myself and my self-esteem. I promise to stay committed to these goals and, in turn, reward myself when I meet a goal. I won't feel guilty about my reward. I promise to practice self-care for the term of this contract, which is _____ months."

Continue by breaking down the goals into smaller steps and writing them down, as discussed earlier. You can even make it easier by coming up with a summary of each broken-down goal.

For example, if you want to stop drinking so much soda, your summary could simply be *no soda*. Write it on sticky notes and place the notes in strategic places where you'll easy notice them.

Activity: Worksheet for Realistic Goal Setting

ACTIVITY 3:

Take note of the action verb *will* in the paragraph below. Always set your goal with a definite commitment. Avoid saying that you'll try to do something or that you intend to follow through. Make sure to set a deadline at the end.

Target Declaration: I will…

_____

_____

_____

_____

by _____ , 20 _____ .

ACTIVITY 4:

Implementation plan: I will accomplish this goal through the following steps:

1.

2.

3.

4.

ACTIVITY 5:

Signing is a crucial part of this exercise. Your signature holds you responsible and links you to this task.

Signature activity:

I owe myself this change because _____.

This _____ day of _____, 20___, I pledge to make this improvement in my life.

Signature:

CHAPTER FOUR:
IT IS NOT JUST A TASK

You need to understand that developing your self-esteem is not just a task—it's something that will affect you personally. Self-esteem is important not just in your personal life but also in your day-to-day experiences at school, sports, or a part-time job. Effective communication skills, conflict-management skills, and innovative critical-thinking abilities are three of the top ten attributes that will take you far in life, whether in school, college, or work. And your self-esteem has a significant impact on each of these attributes.

Your capacity to attain skills and knowledge and grow in your chosen area is a reflection of your self-esteem. If you have a good sense of self-esteem, you will be motivated to learn all that you can and stay informed over time. You'll be more motivated to develop the abilities required to stay competitive, which is critical to your capacity to preserve your own personal well-being.

A little confused? Let's break it down by looking at these skills one after the other and analyzing how they are intertwined with your self-esteem.

Developing Communication and Critical Thinking Skills

Conflict and Communication

Your ability to handle and resolve conflicts is closely linked to your self-esteem and self-perception. Suppose you believe that you don't have any helpful knowledge or relevant experiences to offer. In that case, your ability to handle conflict is a lot weaker. If, on the other hand, you feel positive about yourself and have healthy self-esteem, you will be eager to share your thoughts, personal stories, and support to help you handle conflicts and solve problems in your daily life.

Communication can be worsened by low self-esteem. People with low self-esteem often seek time alone. To safeguard their worth, those individuals must believe they have something that no one else does. This might cause them to hide information that might be critical to the process of handling conflicts. They consider it essential to their own safety, even though hiding such knowledge may be costly to the people around them, to society, and to themselves.

If you believe the knowledge you have is worthless, you may not feel compelled to share it, which is another way that self-esteem can worsen communication. Throughout the process of handling conflicts, some knowledge is widely known by everyone, some is known just by a few, and some is known by you alone. Information that you might think is unimportant may actually be critical to resolving the problem, but it can't be accessed by others unless you are willing to share it.

Innovative Critical Thinking

Creative thinking is a life-changing skill. It helps you thrive in situations where others have failed. People with low self-esteem may struggle to believe that their thoughts, opinions, and ideas are valid, and they may shut down the critical thinking and creative areas of their lives. They might begin to follow rather than lead. They frequently accept the word of others rather than establishing their own voice. They prefer to stroll the paved path rather than tromping through the grass and creating their own route.

As your self-esteem improves, you realize that your views, opinions, and creative voice are just as valuable as the next person's. You begin to learn that the more innovative and critical you are in your attitude toward life, the healthier your self-esteem will be since you are mapping your own path rather than simply wandering in the shadows. You have more options if you think innovatively and critically.

Self-esteem is very important for critical thinking. To develop critical thinking skills, you must be confident in your talents, ambitions, and abilities. You have to be able to observe the world around you, sort your emotions, and use discipline while making decisions. This involves being able to recognize your mistakes and tell right from wrong. If you have low self-esteem, you can't do these things because you're too weighed down with self-doubt that makes you second-guess your every action.

It takes a lot of bravery to think creatively. It shows that you're not afraid to try new things. Being inventive and finding fresh answers to old challenges is required for creative thinking.

Creative thinking shows that you are self-assured and unafraid of criticism. Being a clone of other people doesn't sit well with creative minds. Creative people have their own distinctive approaches. Curiosity and the urge to know more and do things differently are also essential components of creative thought. Finally, creative thinking requires greater perseverance than most people are capable of. Only people with healthy self-esteem can develop these traits and take themselves to greater heights.

Curating these skills at a young age will put you at the top of the game as you progress and experience new things in life.

Understanding Change and the Growth that Comes with It

Your readiness to change is closely related to what you believe about yourself and how assured you are in your own abilities. In today's fast-paced, ever-changing world, change happens so quickly that you hardly have time to learn one thing before that knowledge becomes outdated and the world has moved on. Most people are happy to be around others who aren't afraid to adapt, develop, grow, and take chances. This can-do attitude is directly related to how confident you are in yourself.

Your ability to adapt and evolve can greatly enhance your life. If a potential benefactor, teacher, or employer sees how well you can adapt and learn new things, they may be willing to trust you with more responsibility. Change is never simple. Even good or beneficial change can be challenging.

Consider these bits of advice as you strive to become more receptive to change:

- Ask for advice and support.
- Be the kind of person who takes a step in the right direction.
- Consider the overall result.
- View change as an opportunity for development and growth.
- Maintain effective communication channels.
- Maintain an open mind about change and the individuals involved.

Understanding and Solving the Mistakes that Come Along with Change

Your self-esteem influences how you handle adversity, whether it's the result of your own actions or someone else's. Making mistakes is a natural part of life, and many people think of their failures as learning tools. People with low self-esteem, on the contrary, may find mistakes disheartening. They regard them as true failures rather than chances for improvement. They think of mistakes as an endpoint rather than a fresh start. If you consider mistakes to be setbacks, you won't be willing to take chances and risks. When you see a mistake as something you can't overcome, you're less willing to try something new or unusual.

Fear of making mistakes causes you to become stuck. This is a direct result of low self-esteem. People with healthy self-esteem recognize that mistakes are simply good practice for the next time around. They view mistakes as evidence that they are attempting new things and progressing. They regard them as human characteristics shared by everybody. Mistakes can even help you reclaim the part of yourself that forgot it's okay to be imperfect.

Just as self-esteem is important in your personal life, it's also important in your professional life as you progress toward your future career. Healthy self-esteem will help you be more successful in your job, which can lead to a higher salary or better opportunities.

Do you see a chore that has to be done as a hated duty, or do you say a tiny "thank you" because you have the ability and strength to do that particular hated duty? It all depends on your perspective. Your self-esteem influences how you experience and understand things in the world around you.

Skills You Need to Improve Your Self-esteem

Seven primary factors form the foundation for social and emotional development and, as a result, contribute to healthy self-esteem. The link is mutual—healthy levels of self-esteem allow for the development and improvement of these seven factors. With adequate support, the seeds sowed in childhood should continue to develop and, hopefully, bloom throughout adulthood into these skills.

1. **Self-Knowledge**
   - Cultivating a strong sense of self, an awareness of who you are and where you fit into your environment
   - Understanding distinctions and similarities, how you vary from others in appearance and personality, and the characteristics you share with them

- Understanding how you react differently from other people when in similar situations

2. **Understanding Myself and Others**
- Understanding how relationships operate—namely, being able to build and retain your own uniqueness as a separate individual while acknowledging the inevitable interdependence of relationships
- Understanding the problems that come with relationships and learning to work together
- Seeing things from another person's point of view and gaining an insight into how they could perceive you
- Learning to appreciate and tolerate other people's points of view
- Understanding your emotions and being aware of the ways in which you express them
- Knowing that you can choose how to express your feelings
- Understanding other people's feelings and distinguishing your own feelings from those of others

3. **Self-Acceptance**
- Identifying your own abilities and noticing areas where you struggle and desire to improve
- Accepting that making mistakes is inevitable and that this is frequently how we acquire knowledge
- Knowing that you are doing your best with the information and abilities you have
- Being satisfied with your physical appearance

4. **Self-Reliance**

- Knowing how to look after yourself
- Recognizing that life is frequently challenging, but there are many actions you can take to help pave the way
- Developing a sense of freedom and self-motivation
- Ability to self-monitor and alter your behaviors, attitudes, and thoughts in response to your progress toward goals
- Believing that you are in control of your life and can handle challenges and crises as they come your way

5. Self-Expression
- Understanding how we interact with one another, not just via words but also with facial expressions, body language, inflection, clothing, and so on
- Exploring how to read the cues beyond the words so that you may better understand people and express yourself completely and consistently
- Acknowledging and appreciating the many ways in which we can express ourselves.

6. Self-Confidence
- Knowing that your views, beliefs, and actions have worth
- Understanding that you have the liberty to be yourself and that your presence matters
- Adopting a unique strategy of problem-solving and having enough confidence in your own talents to explore various problem-solving techniques and skills
- Being adaptable enough to switch up your methods and strategies if they don't work
- The ability to take on problems and make decisions

7. **Self-Awareness**
- Developing the ability to stay in the present moment rather than being consumed by negative thinking or emotions about the past or future
- Knowing your own abilities and learning to create reasonable but challenging goals
- Recognizing that emotional, mental, and physical change are all normal parts of your existence
- Recognizing that you have a say in how you adapt and progress
- Being confident enough in yourself to devise techniques for effectively dealing with the unpredictable

This list may seem overwhelming, but it's not difficult to develop these skills to some extent. These skills will go a long way toward helping your self-esteem and overall personal development.

Getting the Job Done

Getting the work done is a reasonable but demanding expectation to have for yourself. It's an important step that frequently gets overlooked. It takes practice and effort, just like any other skill you want to cultivate. If you recall, we covered how difficult change can be and some of the reasons for this earlier in the chapter. Setting clear objectives allows us to be in charge of the path to change, which helps us maintain healthy self-esteem.

Fear of failure may discourage some people from setting regular goals for themselves. We are sometimes advised that we won't reach our goals for one reason or another (e.g., not being smart enough, rich enough, etc.). If we hear these things enough times, they may add to our own self-limiting mindset.

We are sometimes motivated to attempt new endeavors, but we fail because we lack motivation or a clear understanding of how completing the objective would change how we feel about ourselves. Getting the job done and reaching our targets is inherently difficult—we risk making mistakes, but we also risk success. Setting overly high targets for ourselves can cause the consequences to appear too great, preventing us from taking the first baby steps.

Considering these factors, it is important to take things step by step and give ourselves a reward when we begin to make adjustments and reach our goals. We often rely too much on praise from key people in our lives, such as parents and best friends. But as we grow older, it becomes increasingly crucial for us to acknowledge and praise our own achievements. We can strengthen our feelings of self-worth with this approach.

So, any goal or job we want to get done for ourselves must first be practical and attainable. We must be specific about our goals and targets and how and when we want to do them. Each objective should be consistent with our views about what is "right" for us, and we must recognize the advantages of fulfilling that goal.

Activity: Past Mistakes

ACTIVITY 6:

The purpose of this activity isn't to force you to focus on your problems. Instead, it's supposed to make you think about times when you made a mistake and couldn't accomplish what you wanted.

For each category listed below, spend some time and find at least one unpleasant event that occurred due to your own mistakes and unwillingness to change.

1. Mistake(s) that affected your family:

_____

_____

_____

_____

2. Mistake(s) that affected your school life:

_____

_____

_____

_____

3. Mistake(s) that affected your social life:

_____

_____

_____

_____

4. Mistake(s) that affected your friends:

_____
_____
_____
_____

5. Mistake(s) that affected your relationships with strangers:

_____
_____
_____
_____

6. Mistake(s) that affected you and your happiness:

_____
_____
_____
_____

ACTIVITY 7:

Now that you've identified at least one mistake in each area, consider how you can learn from each one, and how you would handle the same mistake in the future.

1. What you learned from the mistake that affected your family and how you will better handle the same mistake if it happens again:

_____

_____

_____

_____

2. What you learned from the mistake that affected your school life and how you will better handle the same mistake if it happens again:

_____

_____

_____

_____

3. What you learned from the mistake that affected your social life and how you will better handle the same mistake if it happens again:

_____

_____

_____

_____

4. What you learned from the mistake that affected your friends and how you will better handle the same mistake if it happens again:

_____

_____

_____

_____

5. What you learned from the mistake that affected your relationship with strangers and how you will better handle the same mistake if it happens again:

_____

_____

_____

_____

6. What you learned from the mistake that affected you and your happiness and how you will better handle the same mistake if it happens again:

_____

_____

_____

_____

CHAPTER FIVE:
FINDING AND ACCEPTING
WHO YOU ARE

Before you can ever triumph in public, you must first conquer personal struggles within yourself. Giving up on finding yourself is essentially giving up on your future — your ambitions, objectives, desires, and drive to improve. Self-esteem issues might cause you to lose sight of the future or lose hope that things can and will improve. Even though you're still literally alive, it might lead you to quit really living to the fullest.

Finding yourself starts with how you see yourself before you can start considering how others see you. We crawl before standing. Before calculus, we study basic math. Before we can support others, we need to help ourselves. If you want to change and improve your life, you should start with yourself, not with your parents, friends, boyfriend/girlfriend, teacher, etc. Accepting who you are starts with you. The work is done from the inside out, not from the outside in.

Your self-esteem is similar to a savings account. Let's refer to it as your own savings account. You make cash transactions by either withdrawing or depositing funds into your savings account.

When you are dedicated to finding and accepting yourself for who you are while improving along the way, that is a plus for your self-esteem; that is, you are depositing into your personal self-savings account. When you're in denial about yourself and not committed to finding out the real and genuine you and what you really stand for, that's a withdrawal from your personal self-savings account.

Defining and Finding Your Happiness

The proportion of joy and happiness you let into your life is primarily determined by how you feel about yourself. If you don't believe you deserve happiness, you won't let it come to you. Suppose you consistently believe that happiness is a hopeless case. In that case, you will stop seeking it and will be unable to notice it when it is right there in front of you.

Happiness. That's a very meaningful word on its own! Unless you've not ever experienced it, just hearing or seeing the word makes you feel a bit better. People are frequently misled by the thought that they deserve happiness and joy and that it should come to them without any work or activity on their part. Some people feel that happiness is something they're automatically owed.

Happiness, like love, is immeasurable. You can't hold it or touch it with your fingertips. You can't wrap it up and keep it for later. You lose motivation to fight for something when you can't see it. The same can be said about happiness. When it comes to happiness, one thing is certain—you know when you have it and when you don't.

There are several major causes of unhappiness, the most common of which are unreasonable expectations. Setting high objectives and aiming high is good or even necessary at times. But every desire and aspiration has a limit. Setting unreasonable expectations for yourself is a recipe for misery.

Another source of continuous unhappiness is negative thinking, which is a byproduct of low self-esteem. Negative thinking distorts your perception of yourself, your life, and your prospects for happiness. Another big issue surrounding unhappiness is relying on others for happiness. Other people can't offer you happiness or a strong sense of self. Sure, people play an important part in our self-esteem and happiness, but relying on others for either will ultimately lead to dissatisfaction.

Unhappy people frequently seek solace from friends, relatives, or strangers. You can find short-term relief in other people, but lasting happiness comes from understanding that you are deserving of happiness, that you value yourself, and that you are making a positive impact on the world.

The trouble with seeking happiness in others or relying on others to bring you happiness is that when that person isn't around anymore, they take your happiness with them. You're therefore left with just one option: to be yourself. And if you weren't satisfied with yourself when they were in your life, then you won't be happy after they depart.

Understanding the Path of Self-Acceptance

When we have unhealthy self-esteem, we may strive to hide our true selves from others. However, burying our difficulties doesn't help us solve them. Your self-acceptance has a significant impact on your personal satisfaction. Knowing your personal characteristics might be the difference between being and doing.

If you don't know what you prefer or appreciate, what you cherish, where you excel, how you want to be regarded, and whether you work best alone or with people, you may never be able to truly connect with yourself. Understanding your quirks, bad habits, needs, and intrinsic abilities can also help you make competent career choices that work with your personal interests and passions. As a result, you'll feel better about yourself and your contribution to the world.

Finding your true self and accepting it is as simple as discovering what you are able to achieve. That sentence may sound a little vague, but finding your true self implies that you've discovered the most important parts of who you are inside. For some, they fall in love with art, science, restoring things, or simply being among people. Others enjoy traveling, painting, educating, or dealing with animals. Find that thing that draws you so tightly toward your happiness that you can't fight it, even though many people do!

Listening to what you're telling yourself is just as important as planning where and how your life should go. Maybe you've been in a circumstance where you didn't listen to your inner self, and your judgments, deeds, and preferences contradicted your internal purpose. You will typically be unhappy and unsatisfied when you do this. As a result, your self-esteem weakens. This is why one of the true foundations of good self-esteem is purpose.

Paving and Following the Path to Self-Acceptance

Self-acceptance implies that you have discovered your purpose and that this purpose guides all of your endeavors, ambitions, objectives, and activities. Many people base their sense of self-acceptance or meaning in life on their employment. In contrast, others prioritize material possessions or achievements.

Self-acceptance is more than just a purpose. It is more powerful than another person and more durable than your assets. Your own self will never abandon you. You may abandon your goal of finding yourself, but the part of you that you've accepted will never let you go.

As you deepen your bond with yourself, you'll realize that you are unique and perfect just the way you are. You can open yourself up to whatever happens with unconditional acceptance by befriending yourself and being accepting of your true needs and wants. Throughout this process, you will discover that your fundamental uniqueness is good and pure and that you can be a part of something grander in the world around you.

One method to pave your road toward self-acceptance and finding meaning in life is to evaluate what's going on in the present. Are you happy about the outcomes of your actions? Do your efforts yield the desired results? Do you work more and work harder, yet success remains unattainable? If this is the case, you may not be living your purpose, and you may not be accepting yourself for who you are.

You may be on a path that is not aligned with your life's goal, which might be one of the causes of low self-esteem. If you continue to neglect your purpose, refuse to admit that you have value, and keep doing the same things over and over, you will never understand self-esteem. You may need to explore every avenue open to you to find yourself, your voice, or your purpose.

When you accept and embrace all aspects of yourself and love yourself wholeheartedly, your innate value shines through. You're vulnerable, and without your thick defenses, you can actually be there for yourself and your loved ones. You realize that success and failure come and go as you learn to embrace the shifting nature of everything. When you grasp that your life is a journey, you become aware of a way of responding to yourself that goes beyond the superficial basics.

How can you shift your focus from restrictive acceptance to complete acceptance and compassion? How can you overcome your desire for praise from others, nurture your inner traits, and recognize your intrinsic worth?

The answer is that you start where you are now. You're the only one who has the ability to sow the seeds of conscious self-acceptance during your journey of cultivating healthy self-esteem. You can get your judgmental ideas out of the way, focus on the present moment, and discover that the person you've been seeking has always been there.

How Self-Acceptance is Important to Your Self-Esteem

Let's redirect our focus to our inner self and remember that unconditional love and self-acceptance are essential for mental health and growth, which leads to better self-esteem.

Unconditional love and acceptance mean that we decide to love ourselves despite the things we don't like about ourselves. Personal development is one of life's greatest joys.

There is a common misconception that self-acceptance is the end rather than the beginning of healthy personal growth. As a result, self-esteem is founded on a mix of self-acceptance and growth. Climbing a slope is similar to growing. When you know you're on solid ground, you can push up with confidence and have fun. Some people might try to stop your progress by reminding you of past mistakes or flaws.

Accepting Your Uniqueness

Self-esteem doesn't mean practicing positive thinking in which you tell yourself how magnificent and perfect you are in the hopes of becoming that way. Because it's not anchored in reality, this type of thinking is emotionally weak and exhausting. People that have high self-esteem don't need to exaggerate themselves. Rather, they are confident enough to assess their own strengths and flaws. Self-acceptance begins with an honest assessment of your current state of development. When done with love for your real and genuine self, this approach can be highly self-affirming and positive.

We simply need to acknowledge where we are today with love and without fear. Fear arises when a person assesses their core negatively. What could be more terrifying than realizing that we're never going to be perfect people? But the term *imperfect* is unreasonable since it suggests that we are constantly and completely hopeless.

Don't let your mistakes define you. Don't let criticism, failure to meet goals, prior traumas, lack of money or prestige, or anything else define you. Each individual is far too valuable and complicated to be viewed in such a limited way.

If you're in the process of accepting yourself and your uniqueness, you should consider keeping these ideas at the back of your mind:

- Self-acceptance is a continual process that will never be finished.
- The process of accepting yourself is a method of self-love. It's rewarding because it begins with a stable inner foundation of value and affection.
- Improving and accepting yourself is difficult. Be ready to invest a lot of effort.
- Accepting yourself isn't about competing or comparing. You can choose your own path and speed. It's best to choose a pace that can be maintained for the rest of your life.
- Loving yourself entails loving others as well.
- Because loving yourself is a process rather than a result, you don't need to see results before you experience a boost in self-esteem. You merely need to follow the flow and enjoy the process.

Pose a few questions to yourself. What are your unique abilities? What distinguishing and unique characteristics do you possess? What are you capable of achieving that others are not? What skills and abilities do you have that you don't see used every day? Answering these questions can assist you in discovering your uniqueness and embracing it.

Activity: An Exercise in Mind Rehearsal

Ten Positive and Unique Statements About You	
Statements:	Proof of truthfulness:
1.	
2.	
3.	
4.	
5.	
6.	
7.	
8.	
9.	
10.	

1. Make a list of ten significant, realistic, true, unique, and positive statements about yourself. If you highlight a task in which you excel, attempt to include particular personal attributes that explain why. Instead of merely stating that you are a good listener, you might say that you assess situations quickly and respond decisively. Or, instead of saying you are tidy, you might note that you help out your mom by cleaning for her so that you can reduce her workload around the house. Roles can vary, but character and personality qualities can be exhibited in a variety of roles.
2. Complete the worksheet on the next page with the ten positive and unique statements.
3. Find a quiet area to unwind for 15 to 20 minutes. Consider one statement after the other and think for a minute or two about whether each is really true.
4. Work on these activities over the next ten days. Add an extra statement in the area provided if you think of any.

Additional Statements	
Statements:	Proof of truthfulness:
1.	
2.	
3.	
4.	
5.	
6.	
7.	
8.	
9.	
10.	

CHAPTER SIX:
STEPPING OUTSIDE YOUR
COMFORT ZONE

Your comfort zone is where you feel the most comfortable, protected, and competent. You know what to anticipate and how it feels. Leaving your comfort zone is often frightening since you're confronted with new and unfamiliar situations. But expanding your comfort zone is fairly simple, and once you've done it the first time, it will become second nature.

Even though we all have different comfort zones for various reasons, one thing is certain—we all have things that make us uncomfortable. This chapter is all about supporting you in stepping out of your personal comfort zone and overcoming your worries, concerns, and restrictions. You'll learn to push the limits and go above and beyond to achieve a different level of thinking that can provide you with the life you truly desire!

So, before we move on, take this Zone Test to determine your present comfort zone and pinpoint which areas of your life might be weighing you down, from the obvious ones to those you may not be aware of. This will provide you with a personal framework to work from as well as a higher sense of self-awareness to help you improve.

Because this evaluation is a framework for you and your personal growth, you'll get the most out of it if you address the questions truthfully. Remember that these questions are general and based on self-analysis. It's not a professional evaluation or a psychological assessment. Instead, think of it more as a quick way to figure out more about your comfort zone and where you are in your life.

Skip ahead to the activity portion of this chapter to complete the evaluation before proceeding.

What to Expect When Stepping Out of Your Comfort Zone

When was the last time you did anything that intimidated you? When did you most recently test yourself, take a chance, or push your limits to the point that you broke right through them? Simply put, when was the last time you moved outside of your comfort zone and used it to effect good change in your life?

Haven't you ever wondered what you might accomplish if you stepped outside your comfort zone and pushed your boundaries? If you've ever successfully addressed and overcome a specific fear of doing anything, it's a safe bet that, in that instance, you felt an overpowering sense of freedom, self-worth, and gratifying fulfillment. I'm sure you'll agree that it's a pretty wonderful experience!

For a few seconds, imagine feeling like this all the time—that incredible sensation you get after you've achieved something, as you look your fears in the face and break through your barriers. It's enough to leave you feeling powerful, as if there's nothing in the world that can stop you from accomplishing and obtaining all you desire.

If it were that simple, wouldn't we all just face our anxieties and be done with it? You can't have all that self-gratification for free, which is where the law of giving and taking comes in. There are conditions that come with achieving this feeling.

Moving outside your comfort zone requires you to take risks, be brave, and make unusual choices. You don't have to accomplish it all at once—you can take baby steps to expand your zone.

Assume that you're scared of speaking in front of a group of people, yet you need to develop this ability for college admissions. You don't have to rush to the theater tomorrow. Start by volunteering to read to kids. When you feel more comfortable, offer to appear in front of a small group, such as at a club meeting or a religious event.

Another major aspect of leaving your comfort zone involves learning how to hold back the fear that comes with taking a risk. Addressing your inner fears is a big component of taking risks. Fear may be a motivator for some and a demotivator for others. It's often the thing that prevents people from developing and living. Fear can be a fundamental contributor to low self-esteem. On the other hand, fear can sometimes be beneficial. Fear can help us stay safe by warning us that something is odd, out of place, or just wrong. But irrational fear might drive us to be afraid of things without reason.

By confronting your fears and taking action to conquer them, you begin to improve your life in a variety of ways. First, the fear that had previously immobilized you has vanished. Following that, you begin to feel better about yourself as your self-esteem continues to develop. Facing your anxieties is a valuable strategy for improving your self-esteem.

One of the first steps in embarking on your new adventure is to answer this question: *If I had nothing to lose, what would I do?* This is a powerful question, and it begs for answers. What thoughts did you have? Before you go any further, jot down your biggest dream. It can be written on the side of this page, on the back of the book, or on a paper towel.

Knowing Why You Want to Leave Your Comfort Zone

Envision your comfort zone as a target on a wall. Each circle from the center is broader and includes a bigger space than the one inside it. This is similar to your own personal comfort zones. As a child, your zone is somewhat small.

Your comfort zone expands as you grow older, discover more, and have more life experiences. For some, the zone ends here because they refuse to be open to new options and experiences. They are hesitant to take chances.

Not taking chances can help you avoid pain, frustration, fear, and grief, but it also keeps you from learning, developing, loving, growing, and truly living. Now that you know all the benefits you can get from expanding your comfort zone, you'll wish to expand regardless of the pains that come with it.

Knowing exactly why you want to overcome your boundaries will be your motivator as you go through the pains of leaving your comfort zone. Overcoming challenges and reaching beyond what is accepted or usual are the foundations of healthy self-esteem. It is based on overcoming your fears, anxieties, worries, and self-imposed restrictions.

You have everything you need to start. You've decided to step outside of your comfort zone. You're ready to face your fears and deal with your anxieties. You've evaluated your skills, revived an old dream, and you're ready to take some risks. All you need now is the drive to move forward. All the motivations you need will come from your goals. There are two classifications of motivation: external motivation and internal motivation.

External motivation is the least effective because it's the drive that comes from people pushing you rather than from you pushing yourself—a passion that is fueled by external rewards or consequences. Your parents forcing you to attend college is an example of external motivation. External motivation is artificial and not genuine.

Most desires and objectives are not realized because of external motivators. They are unreachable because they aren't truly yours, and you didn't start them. A dream must be your own; otherwise, it's quite likely that it will not be fulfilled.

Internal motivation is the most powerful motivator since it originates from within you and is motivated by your desire to improve. Internal motivation is a powerful psychological force that compels you to get up and leave. It's uncontrolled energy.

You've experienced it before. It's that unexplainable feeling when you just can't stop yourself from doing something. It's the insatiable desire to grab the bull by the horns and rule the world.

Most aspirations are attainable when motivated by internal or personal motivation.

When you step just a little outside of your comfort zone, it becomes almost addicting to figure out what you can do next. Only you can find the answer.

Taking Baby Steps Out of Your Comfort Zone

Although it's possible for some of us to leap right into tackling our anxieties, a proper warm-up typically leads to better performance and results. It all starts with the right mental preparation.

Let's start with changing how you see and think about things. This is when you can expect to see different outcomes. Consider this example: someone you know has an overwhelming phobia of drowning. However, there comes a moment when a child is drowning in a public swimming pool, and they are the only person around to help. Their fears are still there, but the person acts immediately and dives into the pool to help the child.

In this scenario, if there was someone else available to help the child, the person would have let their fears keep them out of the water. However, in this situation, the desire to save the child was greater and much more important than any fears, and the person's fears naturally moved to the back of their minds as they focused on the task at hand. Aside from the above example, an image you may have seen on television at some point is a person helping whisk a child to safety when a vehicle is about to hit them while playing. This kind of situation frequently occurs during traumatic events such as natural disasters or accidents where our fears are overridden by deeper instincts and personal values.

One of the major motivations people have for taking action are personal convictions and values. They motivate us to act despite fear or danger, which is why it is important to identify and cultivate a strong sense of values in the first place. Responsibility, personal honesty, and integrity are a few traits incredibly important to many people. These are the traits that help us overcome moments of overwhelming fear to do what is right.

The other thing to keep in mind is perspective and focus. In the above situations, the focus is not on the danger but on what will happen if the fear is not overcome. This is something that anyone can apply to smaller, less life-threatening situations.

For example, let's say you would like to become a good dancer, but every time you take a lesson or practice, you fear looking silly and therefore avoid practicing. You might shift your focus to the end result and contemplate what will happen in the long run if you never allow yourself to look silly in the beginning while practicing. If you never practice, you'll never learn how to dance, and feeling silly while new at anything is unlikely to ever change.

So, changing how we think is essential for changing how we feel, and it is via this process that we might suddenly become capable of entirely new behavior. I've previously mentioned some of the methods we can use to accomplish this, but it all starts with adopting a different attitude and way of thinking.

One method of conquering fear and stepping out of our comfort zone is to place ourselves in situations where we have no option but to simply do the things that we dislike. Getting there is about taking baby steps and building resilience to conquer any remaining anxieties.

Another method you can adopt when you're afraid or out of your comfort zone is to ask yourself questions that can help you put things into perspective and take things in stride. In certain circumstances, it can even fix the problem by helping you to get to the bottom of it. You do this by looking beyond the immediate problem and gradually breaking things down in stages.

Self-Assessment Questions

- Is the issue truly important right now? Is it truly that significant in the larger scheme of things? Is it worth compromising my health for this stress/anxiety/fear?
- Would there have been any purpose in being so afraid and wasting time if I died tomorrow?
- Would it make a significant difference if I did or did not stress and worry about this problem right now?
- What good does anxiety do if something bad is going to happen anyway? What is the most effective action I can take to achieve the greatest possible outcome given the circumstances?
- How exactly is this a problem? What is stopping me from finding a solution and moving forward?
- Am I being as creative as I could be? What can I do to help? What advantages do I have at my disposal?
- What can I be thankful for and express gratitude for?

Pretending to be someone else is another method of taking baby steps out of your comfort zone. With this in mind, pretend to be someone you admire for their confidence, fearlessness, or sense of humor, etc. Mirror some of their positive characteristics, including how they physically hold themselves, and consider their ideals and attitude toward things. It's almost like doing an impersonation of them.

You might even choose to model yourself after someone you know and like. Make light of it if it helps you get into the correct frame of mind. If modeling someone sounds intimidating, try doing an impression of a real person or a character from a TV show, movie, or book. Even a basic impression can be enough to transform your attitude and give you the extra push you need to accomplish anything.

Taking Bigger Positive Risks

Our potential to make decisions is critical when it comes to breaking down barriers, stepping outside of our comfort zones, and taking risks. If we're afraid of making the wrong choice or worrying about the possible consequences for too long, it might keep us from making any decisions at all or taking that step forward into unknown terrain.

However, the moment we feel secure about our decision-making process, we open up many more doors of opportunity to push our boundaries even further because every action steers us in that direction.

On the surface, decision-making and risk-taking appear straightforward; they refer to the process of selecting one or two plans of action, and it's something we do every moment of every day. However, as we all know, simple doesn't always mean easy! It gets complicated when we obsess too much over making the perfect decision.

Yet there may not always be a "best" decision among the available options. So, we do the best we can with the available resources and information. We move forward, trusting that whether the decision is right, incorrect, or neutral at the time, we have the skills to adapt.

Risk-taking is naturally terrifying, but it is also one of the essential things you can do to step out of your comfort zone, lower your anxiety about the future, and lessen your concerns about stagnation. Taking risks indicates that you're willing to try new things and be bolder.

Some pointers on taking risks, big or small:

- Ignore your negative thoughts.
- Know and appreciate yourself.
- Understand what you hope to gain from the risk.
- Be willing to take risks and expect the unpredictable.
- Make use of your goal-setting abilities to assist you.
- Don't surrender or back down at the first indication of difficulty or defeat.
- Recognize that not all risks pay off right away.
- Recognize that taking risks is an investment in your future.
- Understand the dangers of taking risks.

From Comfort Zone to Growth Zone

Entering the growth zone requires effort—you must have pushed through all your personal comfort zones to get here. Pushing beyond our own comfort zones is one thing, but what is the difference that allows us to truly feel and act like we're in a growth zone?

People who are in their growth zones think at completely separate levels with a new mindset; this is about more than simply setting goals. It's about achieving your life's purpose and doing what you "want" rather than what you "need" to do to get what you want out of life.

This results in high self-awareness and knowing yourself so well that you can identify your own future path. It's about daring to let go completely and having that unshakeable belief in yourself.

Having a growth-zone personality doesn't mean that you won't feel unhappy, upset, irritated, misunderstood, or vulnerable to your own issues. However, it does indicate that you understand what's happening on your personal journey and why. This significantly reduces how long you allow negative emotions to affect you.

The majority of us have a deep-seated desire for the things we want in life, whether it is conscious, subconscious, or completely beyond our notice. The difficulty arises when we don't always see this reflected in our daily lives or when we lose sight of our goals for whatever reason.

Whatever your end ambition, purpose, and intention may be, whether great or small, it doesn't really matter. The ultimate objective of this chapter is to provide anyone who wants to be armed with the necessary resources to venture outside their comfort zone and accomplish everything they set their minds to. Nothing is impossible if you have a strong sense of self-awareness and the ability to deal with anxiety, fear, and limitations.

Activity: The Comfort Zone Test

ACTIVITY 9:

Choose which of the answers best applies to you.

For self-improvement, when was the last time I made a risky decision or did something terrifying?

- o Can't recall
- o Within the past month
- o Within the last year

If I am provided with the chance to do something risky that makes me really nervous, I will:

- o Escape the situation totally
- o Purposefully put myself forward
- o Come up with a reason to avoid doing the thing I don't like
- o Determine that I'll do it only if I absolutely have to

I have implicit faith in my intuition.

- o Rarely
- o Sometimes
- o Frequently
- o Almost always

Others perceive me as unique or inventive.

- o Rarely
- o Sometimes
- o Frequently
- o Almost always

I find it difficult to make changes.

- Rarely
- Sometimes
- Frequently
- Almost always

Scenario: I am the leader of the organization and must make the painful decision of letting go of one of two workers. One is my sibling, who is competent at their profession but not the greatest. I know their personal situation makes them completely dependent on this employment. The other person excels in their work and has a spotless employment record. Because of that, I'd choose to fire my family member.

- True
- False

I'm now doing everything I can, regardless of difficulties or problems, to live the life I want.

- True
- False

If I genuinely want anything in life, I always find a way to accomplish it or acquire it. I have goals that I am confident I will achieve.

- Rarely
- Sometimes
- Frequently
- Almost always

I'm uneasy when there are changes in routine, unusual settings, or new tasks that I've never done before.

- Rarely
- Sometimes

- o Frequently
- o Almost always

I'm usually not concerned about my mistakes.

- o True
- o False

I have achieved a great, life-changing personal goal.

- o True
- o False

I know I'm competent at what I do, and I appreciate myself. Regardless of what others think of me, I don't need to prove anything.

- o True
- o False

The following is a list of the themes behind each question:

- Personal limits and general personality/life direction
- Self-motivation, putting yourself in a position of strength
- Self-awareness, self-consciousness, confidence, and self-reliance
- Self-assurance, self-awareness, thinking style
- Flexibility and resistance to change
- Emotional reasoning and the need to be loved
- Ambition and seeing solutions, not problems
- Determination, knowing the result, and the strength of an optimistic belief system
- Uncertainty, need for safety and security
- Self-esteem, anxiety, and decision making
- Current situation and predictions
- Judgment

Activity: Your Place in History

ACTIVITY 10:

Sit back in your chair and pretend you're 75 years old today. Make a mental list of all you want to have accomplished in your life. Items might relate to family, friends, career, adventure, relationships, or anything else—whatever your life should be like and what memories you want to have. Fill in the blanks with your biography as though you died at this same age. What exactly do you want it to say? What do you want others to say or write about you? What would you like your reputation to be?

Consider this activity to be a long-term goal commitment. Think big, but honestly. Consider this for a minute before starting to write.

Now that you've written your biography, take time to choose one of the things that you wrote down but haven't achieved yet, something that you believe will have the most significant impact on your life.

That top one thing is: _____.

Will you have to step outside of your comfort zone to achieve this?

- o   Yes
- o   No

The long-term written goal you have now is not for you to abandon after writing. It's for you to develop a plan of action that will help you achieve this goal. Your goals and objectives will change as you progress in life and experience new things. You can modify the goal as needed but never throw it away. It will serve as a reminder in case you forget where you're headed.

CHAPTER SEVEN:
PERSONAL RESPONSIBILITY

Bearing personal responsibility for your actions might be challenging, but it's an essential component of healthy self-esteem. Recognizing your own actions, whether good or bad, is essential for taking control of your life. You may wonder why somebody would refuse to accept responsibility for their actions. People are accountable for their own judgments, which are frequently unreasonable.

Most people who refuse to accept responsibility for their actions have rationalized their actions in their thoughts. The inability to take responsibility is frequently motivated by self-survival. Some people refuse to accept responsibility because they fear taking a loss if they acknowledge the reality of an action or misunderstanding.

They may fear severe punishments such as physical harm coming to them or even imprisonment. Or they may fear lesser yet, painful repercussions such as a break-up or losing a relationship they care about. In other cases, there are no real risks in taking responsibility, but the person has practiced avoiding responsibility out of fear enough times in the past to now have a habit formed.

Think of a child that has one angry relative that spanks and other relatives that are laid back. Say the child breaks a favorite antique of the angry relative and is yelled at and spanked. In the future, even though the child knows the other relatives do not spank or yell, they may fear taking responsibility again for breaking anything.

Teens and adults work in similar ways. This is why self-awareness is such an important skill to cultivate. If you can recognize patterns within yourself, then you can start to work out why you do the things you do and what you can do to change your unhealthy reactions or habits. Just remember, even if you don't like a certain way you are acting—you've learned to respond in that manner for a reason. At some point or another, that response helped you survive some sort of situation. It's important not to be mean to yourself even when evaluating and changing traits you'd like to improve.

Committing to Personal Responsibility

One significant distinction between humans and other primates is that only humans can be held morally and personally accountable for their actions. Others accepting you as someone who is a responsible person usually means more than just holding a certain belief about you; it's a way of acknowledging that you're willing to change your behavior to fit key situations.

Many individuals identify taking personal responsibility with misconduct, as mentioned before. According to this viewpoint, people usually raise questions about who is responsible and who should be blamed for a mistake. Similarly, we don't always want to own up to what we've done because we're afraid of being punished for breaking from expectations and social norms.

Such a viewpoint contributes to the largely negative habit of promising to find out who's responsible for mistakes or swearing to make someone pay. Other people who embrace a broader idea of personal responsibility link owning up to their own actions with pleasant emotions like thankfulness, respect, and praise instead of always viewing them negatively. They're able to show compassion and love to those who choose to take up their responsibilities because they have been there and understand what it's like.

To understand the viewpoint of someone who is committed to taking responsibility, imagine that you get home from school and notice that your neighbor's tree has fallen down. You never liked that particular tree because it's in the way of your window, so you weren't able to get a nice view of the yard. Your emotions will likely differ based on what you later discover about the cause.

If you want to be gracious instead of blaming, you'll go tell your neighbor that the tree fell and make sure that they don't need any help. You wouldn't just immediately jump to the conclusion of "serves them right" because you disliked how their tree blocked your window.

If you consider this example, since you're not even at fault for the tree falling, it might seem like a strange example of taking responsibility. But what you're really doing is acknowledging that you'll feel better if you take the responsible action of helping your neighbor instead of the negative option of being resentful about the tree. If you don't tell your neighbor, you're punishing them unfairly.

In other situations where you may have wronged someone, taking responsibility allows us the room to fully learn the lessons needed to cultivate strong values. During the moment, taking responsibility might not feel good, but those temporary bad feelings will help you prevent from repeating mistakes in the future. Likewise, taking responsibility will prevent feelings of guilt from lingering, which can have a long-term impact on your self-esteem. By taking responsibility for our actions and trying to make amends when we are in the wrong, we can rest assured that we did everything in our power to keep true to what we think is right.

Avoiding taking responsibility can have a harmful, long-lasting impact on your self-esteem and relationships with others. You can't have healthy self-esteem if you refuse to accept responsibility for your actions, which includes being able to see when you're being unfair to others and making it right. Even if you "get away" with something in the short term, there are invisible repercussions that can affect you and the people around you. For example, it can harm your reputation with your friends and family, which will cause harm to your self-esteem in the long run.

Furthermore, if you refuse to accept responsibility for your faults, mistakes, and incorrect assumptions, you also aren't able to accept credit for your victories, successes, and achievements. This lowers your self-esteem even more. According to the rule of cause and effect, every action has a reaction. This suggests that there is a repercussion for everything you say, do, or think. Ignoring this fact leads to people avoiding their obligations since they don't believe that their actions have any effect.

Handling Self-Blame and Criticism

To some extent, self-blame is just another type of fear. If we can learn to regulate our concerns, we can overcome our problems as well. Imagine you're in charge of a professional group of athletes, and you need to make a critical and defining decision about whether or not to allow someone else to join despite their poor relationships with some players. Looking at things objectively rather than emotionally will make a significant difference in the outcome. Understand that you can't blame yourself if something goes wrong.

Training your mind and way of thinking is the disciplined practice of making sure that you utilize the optimum amount of brainpower you are capable of in any given situation. Thinking's ultimate purpose is to "find out the layout of the terrain." We all have a number of things to consider.

- What is the truth about this situation?
- Are they attempting to exploit me?
- Is it true that they care about me?
- Is it possible that I'm deluding myself into believing what they say?
- What is the best approach to preparing for something I want to do?
- How can I improve my performance?
- Is this my main issue, or do I need to concentrate on something else?

Resolving and finding a solution to those questions is something we have to do every day. That's why we're thinkers.

Self-blame is an ineffective control method. We can't find fault with ourselves. Every day, we are subjected to circumstances beyond our control. Behavioral self-blame is an unhealthy attempt to meet a true, primal need for survival and mental protection. When we suffer a direct hit and blame ourselves, we lose touch with what's really true.

Of course, nothing you do guarantees that you will discover the entire truth about anything or that you won't make mistakes, but there is a way to improve your chances. Improving your reasoning skills and training your mind are real possibilities. However, in order to improve the quality of your thinking, you must learn how to be an effective critic of your own ideas; you can't base your thinking on what others think. And in order to become an effective critic of your own thinking, you must prioritize learning at all times.

Admitting and Overcoming Your Weaknesses

Many people will point out your flaws, insecurities, deficiencies, and mistakes. Once they recognize your flaws, they will use this information against you at every step. They become ruthless in their use of this weapon to exploit you. The best way to overcome this is to be comfortable with recognizing your own flaws and weaknesses, removing the opportunity for others to use them against you.

Suppose you ever lie to someone, and that person discovers it. In that case, that person would have control over you until you reveal the lie to others and own up to lying. By doing so, you deprive the individual who is aware of the deception of their authority over you. You take the power back from that person by confessing.

A weakness is simply something you need to improve upon. It's a shortcoming you might have. Your weakness might be that you lack tolerance, have an attitude, dislike being around infants, or talk too much. Weaknesses aren't permanent, but they are firmly ingrained in your personality and will require a serious effort to change. Suppose you learn that someone is exploiting one of your shortcomings, but you never do anything about it. In that case, your self-esteem, as well as your work and relationships, may deteriorate.

However, imagine that you're the first to acknowledge your weakness. In that case, no one can use that knowledge against you because it's already public knowledge. It's alright to let go of the idea that you're perfect and without weaknesses. You are not, and neither is anybody else. Everyone has both talents and limitations. The trick is to recognize both. Only when you refuse to accept your flaws and failings can another person use them against you. You've made a significant step in removing negative power from others by having the guts and self-esteem to respond, "You're right. I'm not perfect and never will be."

Personal flaws exist. What you consider a weakness, others may consider a gift. What one individual perceives as a flaw in their life, another may perceive as a benefit. Many people have wonderful traits and tremendous talents, but they focus on their one or two flaws and weaknesses. They struggle to get past their weaknesses and focus on their talents. Shortcomings are exactly that—they are temporary. They are not disastrous, life-threatening problems. Our flaws, or perceived flaws, are frequently the product of comparisons to other people and their lives.

It may appear that overcoming your weaknesses is difficult, but it's not. People do it all the time. You've probably conquered several weaknesses without even realizing it.

If you had a friend who needed support and assistance, whether physically, emotionally, or psychologically, you would immediately go to that person. You must now accept that you are a friend to yourself and that you need some extra care and love from time to time. Some techniques you can use to restore and soothe yourself are as follows:

- Find something you enjoy doing and plan time to do it.
- Provide for your body's fundamental necessities (e.g., food, shelter, rest, intimacy).
- To calm your body even more, have a massage, study yoga, or meditate.
- Surround yourself with positive, encouraging people.
- Give yourself permission to develop emotionally, spiritually, and intellectually.
- Take some time away from self-criticism and negative self-talk.
- Take a vacation from the criticism and negative feedback of others.

Other ways to work on your weaknesses include:

- Imagine your life without the observed weakness.
- Set attainable goals to overcome your flaws.
- With each activity and encounter, work toward that goal.
- Tell people about your efforts to tackle this weakness.
- Catch yourself not doing the "thing," and praise yourself.
- Don't become obsessed with this one weakness.
- Don't engage in self-defeating behaviors to overcome the weakness.

Restarting Your Relationship with Yourself

Take some time now to consider yourself in your pursuit of healthy self-esteem. Allow no negative thoughts, emotions, or acts from the past to enter your frame of mind. Consider the positive aspects of your life, your feelings, and your conduct, and reflect on the following questions to help you begin your journey:

- What is your favorite pastime?
- What is your favorite album?
- What is your favorite documentary?
- Where is your favorite spot?
- What is the most reasonable thing you've ever done for yourself?
- What is the most selfless thing you've ever done for another person?
- What is your greatest achievement?
- What are you most grateful for?

Don't stop there. You know yourself better than anybody else. Continue on. Consider your life to be a beautiful tale that has to be shared. No one needs to know, so don't be shy or embarrassed to tell yourself.

Letting Go of Perfectionism

Personal responsibility, blame, lack of purpose, and criticism all share characteristics with perfectionism. They may appear to be detached and abstract from one another, yet they are not. Perfectionism is sometimes the source of blame and the refusal to accept responsibility. If you have perfectionist inclinations, you might be less inclined to accept responsibility for anything that went wrong. It's against your nature to admit you were incorrect or have caused a problem, so you may prefer to blame others in order to avoid the impression of being flawed or inadequate.

Perfectionists share characteristics such as the relentless pursuit of unrealistic goals, never being satisfied with the work done, and believing that a less-than-perfect task equals a less-than-perfect person. They also have an unrealistic fear of failure and the false belief that perfection is linked to self-worth.

Consider the following suggestions if you consider yourself a perfectionist and wish to work on being more honest and compassionate with yourself:

- Rethink your objectives and make them more attainable.
- Recognize that perfect is only a term, not a real possibility.
- Take pleasure in your everyday triumphs and victories.
- Learn to enjoy the process of making mistakes.
- Recognize both your faults and your strengths.

Activity: Finding Closure

ACTIVITY 11:

This activity is put together to help you find closure with two individuals in your life: someone you've used a weakness against in the past and someone who has used your weakness against you in the past. Only think of situations when neither of you apologized. First, write down the names of the two individuals.

The person whose weakness you used against them:

The person who used your weakness against you:

Recognizing unique and valuable qualities in others is an important element of forgiveness. Individuals with healthy self-esteem can perceive these abilities and traits in others and learn from and acknowledge them. Fill in the blanks with at least two positive characteristics about these two people.

Make a list of the good, valued attributes you notice in the first person:

Make a list of the good, valued attributes you notice in the second person:

Find two notecards or pieces of stationery and compose a handwritten note to each person recognizing their positive qualities. If you like, you can make apologies or declarations of forgiveness, but keep in mind that your note must be positive.

Spend time taking notes and reviewing what you said about the people you named. Continue only once you've written both notes.

Was it simple to write the notes?

Yes or No

Can you bear the thought of mailing the notes?

Yes or No

What impact might this have on your self-esteem?

CHAPTER EIGHT: JUDGING YOURSELF WITH FAIRNESS

It might be grueling to assess yourself objectively. So much of our self-perception is influenced by how others view us. However, it will be helpful to understand how to see yourself for who you truly are and not allow anyone to tell you differently.

If you're the kind of person who doesn't judge other people harshly, talk down to them, or try to walk in their shoes before making judgments, you might find this a little easier than people who judge others harshly. It all comes down to not seeing yourself and your accomplishments in a demeaning way, not talking down to yourself, and trying to give yourself a second chance when you make mistakes.

For example, criticizing and demeaning yourself because you don't have a good enough grade is a matter of perspective. Try seeing it this way: If it were a friend who came to you crying and berating herself because of her bad grades, you would probably sit her down and help her understand that receiving a bad grade can happen to anyone. It doesn't make her less of a human.

Finding someone with better grades to help her study might be a solution to that problem.

If you can do that with a friend, what's stopping you from acting this way with yourself? Doing this would change the way you see yourself, better your life, and let you see things realistically for what they are.

Looking at Yourself Through Other People's Eyes

It's human nature to aspire to be better in some way. Everyone has subtle and significant habits that must be broken, attitudes that must be adjusted, and weaknesses that must be strengthened. One method is to ask for opinions from people you trust to see yourself through their eyes.

However, you should know that not all of your friends are necessarily skilled at providing constructive feedback and criticism. Although they may mean well, they might use unsuitable words and phrases or give you comments at an inappropriate moment. When striving to improve your actions and habits through feedback, keep in mind that you may not always receive the desired reaction. Some people may be more forthcoming than you want them to be.

As a result, you must be prepared to listen to what they say. It all comes back to the adage, "If you have the guts to ask the question, you must have the fortitude to hear the answer." Hearing unfavorable views about yourself from others may be quite damaging to your self-esteem. Their criticism fuels your self-doubt, intensifying old worries and driving you to fret about new ones. You must be attentive to what they're saying and understand that you have influence over how you react to and cope with that knowledge.

However, keep in mind that not every comment is accurate. You must view comments as a tool to help you better your weaknesses, not as the be-all and end-all answer. Other people's views are simply that—their views. You may appreciate their perspective, but you will still need to filter through their remarks.

Consider what they say, determine whether they were being fair, think about the context in which their comments were delivered, and then decide whether to accept and act on that input. Seeking feedback on habits, behaviors, attitudes, and activities that you want to change is a good idea. It demonstrates that you have the bravery to ask for advice. Keep in mind, though, that you have the last say on what is real and false in your life.

We can learn a lot from others. We may learn from their mistakes, failures, and accomplishments. However, we can only learn if we're prepared to listen to their comments on an honest level and allow people the opportunity to be openly critical of our work without fear of revenge, violence, rage, or loss of relationships.

People with the highest self-esteem are those who embrace constructive criticism from others. They can distinguish between useful, constructive input and meaningless, self-serving, or harmful comments and feedback.

Putting Things into Perspective

Although everyone is inherently worthy, not everyone has an impression of their own worth. One explanation is that negative and sad thinking patterns can undermine one's self-esteem.

Consider the following scenario: As you walk down the hallway, your teacher scowls at you and a friend. *Oh, no!* you think as you begin to feel low about yourself. *He's annoyed with me. Did I do awful on my test?* But your friend is simply curious, not upset. She assumes that your teacher is just having a bad day or arguing with the principal again.

What's the distinction between the two of you? It's not the incident itself but rather how differently you and your friend interpreted it. Dwelling on the bad nullifies the positive.

In some cases, we actually eliminate positives in order to maintain our low self-esteem. For example, if someone compliments your effort, you might say, "Oh, that was really nothing. Anyone could have done that." You dismiss the reality that you've worked long and hard. It's no surprise that your successes aren't enjoyable. You could have just thanked the person while telling yourself that you do deserve recognition for all the work you do. You would give praise and acknowledge where credit is due to a loved one or friend. Why not do the same for yourself?

Another person's efforts and accomplishments aren't always better just because they're different from yours. To explore this, pay attention to the things people complain about in regard to themselves. You might be surprised to find that people often are oblivious to the things they are good at and are only aware of the qualities they lack. For example, someone you appreciate for being artistic might take their creative skills for granted and instead only sees the things they are not good at. If you pay attention to this, it usually becomes obvious that, in general, people do not have accurate perceptions of themselves. By you noticing where your perception is focused on the negative instead of the positive, you may be able to help others around you see themselves more clearly, too.

Balancing What People Say and What You Choose to Believe

If your teacher positively critiques your performance, consider whether their feedback is valid and truthful. Examine your heart and mind, and honestly answer that question. Only when you refuse to answer the question honestly will you get into trouble. Did you give it your all? Did you stick to the rules? Did you finish it in time? Was it properly formatted? Were there any errors? You must own your truth in this situation. If the fact is that you didn't give your all and didn't get a good grade as a result, then accept it, learn from it, and move on. There's nothing else you can do to change the present.

On the other hand, you might be criticized for your research when you know deep within you that you did exactly what should be done, met the target dates, correctly formatted the report, and met all the other criteria. If your teacher is just being picky for no reason, then the only option is to ignore the criticism and move on. Dwelling on it will do nothing but harm your self-esteem.

Many things affect our self-esteem—from parents to friends, music to professors, criticism to previous mistakes and successes. Everything impacts who you are and how you live your life. These influences are equivalent to a closet full of clothes. You have an option when it comes to deciding what to wear on a daily basis. So, you also have a choice on what impacts your mind and well-being.

Handling Criticism and Compliments

We all like being praised, and we all value helpful advice. But only a few of us, if any, appreciate being put down and subjected to harsh, vicious criticism. Unfortunately, both have an impact on your self-esteem. Some might respond, "Ignore the criticism and revel in the praises." This isn't a healthy mindset. You must either embrace and balance both praise and criticism as learning opportunities or dismiss both as pointless in your life.

If you simply accept compliments and ignore criticism, you're depriving yourself of crucial lessons that may be learned through constructive criticism. Constructive criticism is valuable, practical, and valid advice. It's a critique based on facts, experience, and expertise. "Your paper was well written but needs more depth on the second page," for example, is an example of constructive critique.

But if someone said, "I don't know why we even let you open your mouth in that presentation," then it's clearly not constructive. Nothing can be learned or gained because the criticism is solely meant to hurt your feelings.

Why do you have to accept constructive criticism? Only accepting compliments stunts your progress and makes you content with substandard work. This will not help you develop healthy self-esteem. A person with healthy self-esteem embraces constructive criticism and praise since they are both parts of the learning process.

However, you must be careful not to dismiss the compliments and dwell on the criticism either. This can cause you to reinforce low self-esteem. You might get 100 compliments and a single point of feedback and still go home thinking about the criticism. You let it consume you or dominate your thoughts and actions.

Owning and learning from constructive criticism is the best approach. Ignore it and move on if it is spiteful criticism. You have to pick the most appropriate option based on the circumstances.

Learning to Place Your Self-Worth Above What People Believe About You

Unconditional human worth indicates that you are significant and valuable as a person from the moment you're born. This is the core of who you are on a basic fundamental level. Over time, external factors start to affect how you see yourself as you grow up and learn more about the world around you. You lose sight of this core value that's a part of you no matter what.

For example, mistakes or criticism can mask the core, making it difficult to recognize and feel your own worth. The affection of others makes us feel worthy as well. One method to convey worth is to share your talents. These impact the way worth is perceived rather than the worth itself. If your worth is equivalent to your grades or your relationship, how will you feel when you discover you got a bad grade or that your partner wants to break up?

Your emotions would most likely extend beyond the natural and reasonable grief and disappointment. When your worth is questioned, depression frequently follows. That's why you shouldn't tie your worth to superficial things. Your worth must be basic and unchangeable regardless of outside events or situations.

We distinguish here between feeling guilty about something and feeling horrible about your true self. Guilt over making a mistake can be a good motivator for improvement. Condemning the core of who you are, on the other hand, will only crush your motivation. It's also a good idea to differentiate unpleasant sensations caused by disappointment, sickness, weariness, hormonal swings, rage, fear, and so on from feeling bad about who you are on a core level.

Activity: The Reflecting Activity

ACTIVITY 12:

As you reflect on your readings, which attribute(s) do you value the most that struck out to you immediately?

The attribute(s) I give myself the greatest credit for are...

If an unbiased observer took the time to see you as you are right now, what aspects of yourself do you think they would most appreciate?

What I discovered and learned from this chapter is...

CHAPTER NINE:
BREAKING PAST
FEAR AND JUDGEMENT

Fear exists in all of us, human or animal. We immediately respond to threats with natural defense mechanisms when we know we need to protect ourselves from danger. One thing is certain in life—we all have fears, which is really a good thing because we wouldn't be alive otherwise!

We're talking about innate fear here, the fight-or-flight reaction that is hardwired into us and ultimately helps to protect us. This response causes our bodies to release a flood of adrenaline, allowing us to flee, hide, or fight for our lives.

We all feel fear instinctively, the type of fear that propels us ahead and allows us to progress and flourish. This is the sort of fear that aids in the development of resilience. It should never be interpreted negatively since we are alive, evolving beings, and fear will always be present. It's frequently confused with anxiety, but this kind of fear is only the physical sensation of our minds alerting us to focus.

However, it is important to be conscious of when this natural fear becomes unnatural, illogical, and out of control, holding us back rather than driving us ahead. For example, it's entirely natural to be afraid of losing a loved one, but being anxious about them every day, watching their every move, feeling terrified, and fearing our own sadness — that's a concern!

So, each unwanted or negative emotion may be traced back to fear. Let's start with a typical example: anxiousness. Anxiety about anything, like passing an exam, is likely to stem from a fear of failing, not being good enough, or not achieving what we desire. So, whatever our basic reason for being apprehensive about the exam in particular, it ultimately comes back to fear.

No matter how weak the correlation between fear and other anxiety appears to be, anything that results in an unwanted or bad emotion can be linked back to fear.

Holding Fear at Bay

Everything appears to be driven by fear, and to make matters worse — we're all becoming adapted to it. Most of us aren't consciously aware of the intensity of this present psychological fear, but it's creeping in unconsciously and becoming the norm, despite the fact that the reality is completely different.

This persistent drip feed of fear spinning around and around in your head presents some significant difficulties. It is mostly subconscious, yet it results in the hormonal changes that influence our emotions and eventually contribute to a sense of constant uneasiness that many people endure without knowing why. You know you're feeling sad, unmotivated, upset, or angry, but you don't know the reason why. Does that sound familiar? What can you do to address your fear?

It all begins with changing how and what we think. This is because our ideas influence our emotions, which in turn impact our behaviors, physical health, and the outcomes we achieve in life. There are no boundaries to what we can do once we positively modify our thoughts and responses instead of giving in to fear.

Finding the Motivation to Move On

You will be able to progress and maintain your motivation if you sincerely feel that what you're doing is important, that you are capable of achieving it, and that the ultimate result is worthwhile. Undoubtedly, you will continue to encounter difficult situations, and temporary setbacks may occur.

But having increased your self-esteem will make it simpler to learn from the experience and move on. Remember that if you can't change the circumstance, thinking about it in a new light might help you develop an effective coping plan. This will have an advantageous impact on your confidence.

Some individuals, for example, may still react to you as though you haven't changed at all. Or they may compliment you on your newfound confidence while expecting you to revert to your old habits that were associated with unhealthy self-esteem.

They may continue to take responsibility for tasks you now feel capable of performing independently. Many people have had their progress delayed unintentionally by well-meaning friends and relatives. This won't happen if you can respond assertively to any attempts to entice you back into your previous patterns.

Forgiving Yourself and Moving On

Forgiveness is a matter of the heart. It is both simple and difficult. Forgiveness is about letting go of your pride in order to go on with your life and accepting your own flaws and failings so that you can see both sides of an issue more clearly.

Forgiveness is not only for the other person but also for you. It's making a promise to let go of any negative feelings and focus on the positive as you move forward. You're also making a commitment that you won't cause harm to anyone else by using their shortcomings against them.

Identifying and Pursuing Your Purpose

What do you hope to find within the pages of this book? Is it your life's purpose? Is it your inner self? Is it even possible to find these things? Many specialists on the subject feel that your purpose has always been with you since birth. They believe that your mission is as natural as your hair color or skin tone.

If you haven't found it yet, your life's purpose is extremely important in your pursuit of healthy self-esteem. It may guide you toward your aspirations and objectives, and it can be a guiding force in how you treat others and yourself. It can be a decisive element in the specific role you play in this world.

Finding your life's purpose may be as simple as asking yourself one question: "What do you need?" This isn't the same as what you want. Your needs are quite strong, and they may contain the key to discovering your purpose. There are clear differences between need and want. To demand something, you must have a strong desire for it. Needs are greater than wants. Many people mix up the two.

Needs include things that are necessary to help you live and those that are required to help you live well. Basic needs include oxygen, water, safety, love, and esteem. There are higher-level intellectual demands and, lastly, the desire for self-actualization or self-fulfillment. These are organized in a pyramid commonly known as Maslow's hierarchy of needs. By conducting a quick search online, or even asking a teacher, you can learn more about the common needs every person requires to feel safe and satisfied, which can help you determine what is most important to you.

Activity: Make Your List of Needs

ACTIVITY 13:

Consider what you truly need in your life. Do you need satisfaction? Do you need joy? Do you need compassion? Do you need stimulation? Is it necessary to have a goal? In this exercise, prepare two lists: one list of the things you need to survive and the other list of the things you need to live as your real self. Don't include wants or wishes.

Was that a difficult task? Examine your list to check if there are any wants on it. Can you tell them apart? If you included items such as a new car, a nicer home, or a supercomputer, you are expressing wants rather than needs. You're on the right track if your list of survival necessities includes items such as food, shelter, clothes, safety, and some money. If your needs list also contains family, friends, passion, and intimacy, you understand it correctly.

Consider your list of needs for a moment. Look for common denominators on your list, such as people, power, the desire to go outside, the need to have creative access, or the need to be needed. This will assist you in defining and finding your purpose.

Activity: What If?

ACTIVITY 14:
Reflect on your past. Consider your school life, friends, family, and even distant relatives. What do you most regret doing to someone when you lacked confidence and let fear take over? Did you tell them the true situation? Did you deceive them in any way? Have you betrayed them with your behavior because you were afraid? Fill in the blanks with your answers to the following questions:

Who was harmed as a result of your lack of confidence?

What were their feelings toward you at the time?

What exactly did you do to them?

Why did you choose fear at that point?

What reasons did you give for your actions?

What would you do differently now as you look back?

What would you do differently and positively if the same event occurred right now?

What effect did this action have on your relationship with this person?

What effect did this action have on your self-esteem?

Take out some writing material and compose a confession letter to this person. Explain to them what you did, why you did it, and how you've suffered as a result. Then apologize for causing them suffering due to your lack of confidence. You're not required to give this to the person. Only you can decide how essential this confession is to your self-esteem and your capacity to heal from the past.

CHAPTER TEN:
SELF-ESTEEM FOR LIFE

Unfortunately, nothing will last forever, including self-esteem. You're likely to find yourself at a standstill and even regressing if you don't try to maintain practices that encourage good self-esteem. Self-esteem is not a permanent or continuous state. It must be cultivated, encouraged, fine-tuned, and assessed periodically. Your self-esteem is almost like a newborn that needs to be monitored and cared for in order to grow.

As stated throughout this book, there are several factors that influence your self-esteem. Influences come in many shapes, sizes, and origins—from your parents to your friends, your classmates to strangers, and even your natural desires. Fighting negative self-talk, harsh and unsupportive people, and opponents who would use the power of words and authority to criticize you at every step takes strength. However, you now understand that you have the authority to create your own judgments and the ability to maintain an optimistic outlook on life.

Hopefully, you've examined your life from several perspectives and made some decisions that will help you on your path to good self-esteem. The task at hand now is to maintain the progress you've achieved. The task will be to safeguard the new life you've carved out for yourself from the shattered edges of the past. Working on your self-esteem is now a task you have to work on for life!

You Are Your Number One Support

While it would be amazing to have the support of those you care about, you will realize today that you don't need it. Don't worry about others as you're focusing on improving your grades or getting accepted to a good school. If you want to start looking for a new job, continue researching. Move on if you want to get rid of toxic individuals in your life. You have that control, you have that leverage, and you have that responsibility. You will pledge today to never wait for approval from another individual. Stand and cheer for yourself first.

Today, you will make a promise to yourself to move forward with or without the help, counsel, or approval of others. Self-esteem will always be a considerable challenge. The slope has become far less steep now that you have the skills to develop and safeguard yourself. You have the power, and only you have the influence, to make your life work for you. Choose joy, tranquility, integrity, and forgiveness. Your decisions will change the course of your life forever.

Yes, you've experienced moments that you would rather forget. You've picked yourself up when you've fallen and brushed yourself off more times than you can count. But you succeeded. You did it. You're on your feet and ready to go again!

You are the only person on the planet who has the ability to accomplish this for yourself. You are the only person who has the power to make this happen. As you read through this chapter, you'll be reminded of advice and tactics for looking ahead while working toward greater self-esteem. You won't be able to use every suggestion every day, but it's recommended that you return to this chapter whenever you feel unmotivated, depressed, challenged, threatened, unhappy, or confused.

Finding the Gift and Joy in Every Day

Every person on the planet has a gift that should be shared and ways to put positivity back into the world. Maybe this is as basic as replacing a tire for someone who's broken down on the side of the road. Perhaps it is complimenting a classmate's clothing.

Some effortless, everyday gifts that you may give to others include:

- Writing a weekly message to someone.
- Complimenting a stranger.
- Shopping at auctions for books to donate.
- Offering your pet to participate in a "petting program" at a nursing home or hospital.
- Saving your spare change all year to use for holiday gifts for a charity.

These selfless acts of giving cost little or nothing, but the benefits to those who receive them are great, as are the feelings of joy that you feel.

Lastly, don't forget to reward and give to yourself. You won't be able to nurture the needs, desires, and passions of others if you don't nurture your own. Giving to yourself entails identifying your own requirements for a good existence. Is it true that you require the company of wonderful friends? Do you need your family? Do you need peace and quiet? Do you want to relax with a book and your favorite music?

Do you need to be working, contributing, and assisting others? You have the option of having it all, but you need to plan ahead. For example, you could volunteer one week and focus on yourself the following one.

Saving Significant Cards, Letters, and Mementos

At some time or another, you've probably saved cards, letters, presents, invites, Post-It notes, napkins, and other keepsakes that remind you of good times, nice people, and beautiful moments. If you haven't done this before, it's a great time to start.

Remember that birthday card with a note from a friend that made you stop in your tracks? It stated a couple of things that surprised even you. Where is it? Did you keep it? If you don't already own a box or some safe place in which to put your letters, postcards, and memoranda, go out now and find something that will work.

Start to keep birthday presents, anniversary cards, holiday greetings, personal letters, messages from neighbors, newspaper clippings, quotations, and inspirational tales in this box. When you find something that brings you happiness, put it into the box. This might be a family photo, a snapshot from a magazine or newspaper that reminds you of something good, or a photo from a friend's family.

Your box might contain experiences, thoughts, poetry, and articles that make you pause and reflect on the good things in your life. Perhaps you read a powerful one-line remark that evoked a vivid image. Cut it out, tape it to a piece of paper, then tape it to your box. Remember that your box is a present to yourself for the future, not for today. It's a place to store items that might otherwise be lost or discarded. It's a spot you may return to weeks, months, or even years later. It's a treasure box for your heart.

In addition to your box, you can save things that make you smile or laugh. Keeping a sense of humor improves your self-esteem, stimulates creativity, and reduces stress. You can even write little things that will make you smile when you read them. They can cheer you up when you're sad and motivate you when you're in a slump. You'll be surprised at how quickly your amusing file or memento box can erase the day's unpleasantness and sad memories.

Writing Letters to Yourself

Writing things down has been practiced for thousands of years. Cave paintings show that humans have always wanted to preserve their acts, ideas, and deeds. Writing is a great method of keeping track of your own history. When you start writing, remember that the words are only for you. They won't be made available or publicized in any way. You don't need to be concerned about language, phrasing, or grammar.

Write down your feelings about your experiences. Your notebook does not have to be an expensive leather-bound hardback with fancy lettering. It doesn't have to be a traditional diary with a lock and key. A spiral-bound composition book, loose-leaf writing paper, or a legal pad can all be used.

Writing things down is invaluable. It helps you focus on and heal from the past, make predictions for the future, and converse with yourself. Writing out your feelings might help you feel less anxious and depressed. Writing letters to yourself should be a relaxing experience. You shouldn't be under any obligation to write anything. You don't have to write once or twice a day, but once you start, you might look forward to having a chat with yourself in the late evenings, early mornings, or during lunch.

Your diary might contain everything from your daily thoughts to a letter that you never intend to mail. It might be a letter to an ex–best friend or a letter to a partner you are yet to have. The ideas are unlimited and entirely up to you. Have the following suggestions at the back of your mind as you begin your letters to yourself:

- Don't force yourself to write. It should be your choice.
- If you're stuck for ideas, journal about a quotation or an article you've read.
- Make up a conversation with someone else and see how it progresses.
- Remember to date your entries.
- Keep your diary in a secure location.
- Don't restrict yourself — whatever comes out, comes out.
- Reread your diary on a regular basis.

You will build a healthy habit of keeping track of your emotions, ideas, aspirations, disappointments, defeats, triumphs, and deepest inner workings by communicating with yourself on a daily basis. This is your narrative; write it for yourself.

Activity: Planning Enjoyable Activities

ACTIVITY 15

1. To create an Enjoyable Activities Plan, first, on a separate sheet of paper, write out all of the activities that you have previously experienced and enjoyed. Then, on a scale of 1-10, assess how enjoyable each item was. A score of 1 indicates minimal satisfaction, whereas a score of 10 indicates great satisfaction. We've included a list of ideas on the next page for reference.

2. Next, place a checkmark next to each activity you participated in the activity within the previous 30 days.

3. Circle the activities you'd most likely appreciate doing on a good day.

4. Compare your circled items and your check-marked items. Consider whether there are any activities you used to like that you no longer do.

5. Using the completed Enjoyable Plan list as a guide, prepare a list of 15 activities you want to experience.

6. Make concrete plans to engage in more of these activities. Begin with the easiest and most enjoyable first. Do as many enjoyable things as you possibly can. It would be best if you try a fun thing at least once each day and maybe more on weekends. Many of the things on this list can be used as self-care for difficult days or times in life.

Ideas:

- Spending time with a friend
- Going for a walk
- Completing an art project
- Taking a hot bath
- Exercising
- Completing a puzzle
- Playing a game with family members or friends
- Attending a school event
- Re-organizing your room or school supplies with a creative flair
- Hosting a sleepover
- Attending a concert, play, or film
- Prayer or spiritual practice
- Playing with a pet
- Learning a new skill or hobby
- Listening to your favorite music
- Spending extra time on your hygiene routine
- Reading a good book
- Calling a friend or supportive family member

CONCLUSION

Healthy self-esteem is a lifelong endeavor, and everyone requires assistance along the way. Allow the approaches discussed in the chapters to be your guiding light. As you continue to put what you've learned from this guidebook into practice, ask yourself the self-esteem check questions to see how far you've come and how successfully you're getting rid of negativity! Return to the tasks in the guidebook as needed to aid you along the way.

But please be patient with yourself as you put all you've learned into practice. You won't be able to fix everything overnight and remember that no one does everything perfectly all the time. Perfection is unattainable! Focus on filling your time with realistic and pleasant ideas and feelings, and protect your self-esteem with constructive behaviors.

Remember that a few negative ideas can't take over your self-esteem unless you forget about all the good there is as well. You have the ability to banish those negative thoughts and reframe your mindset to a happier, more positive outlook.

Thoughts of self-esteem to always keep with you:

- I believe in myself.
- I accept myself because I understand that I'm more than my imperfections, shortcomings, or other external characteristics.
- Criticism is an outside force. I look for methods to make progress without assuming that criticism makes me a less valuable person.
- I can evaluate myself without doubting my worth as a human being.
- I observe and appreciate any indication of accomplishment or growth, no matter how minor it may appear to myself or others.
- I admire others' accomplishments and growth without assuming that they are more valuable than I am as a person.
- I am frequently capable of living well and putting in the time, effort, and patience required.
- I believe that people will like and respect me. It's fine if they don't.
- I am aware of and appreciate my own strengths.
- I can occasionally marvel at some of the foolish things I do.
- What I offer has the potential to make a difference in people's lives.
- I appreciate making others happy and am grateful for the time we spent together.
- I consider myself to be a worthy individual.
- I enjoy being a one-of-a-kind person. I'm pleased that I'm unique.
- I enjoy myself regardless of others.

Printed in Great Britain
by Amazon

29818220R00077